A GARLAND OF LOVE

Alice Sharpe

AVALON BOOKS
THOMAS BOUREGY AND COMPANY, INC.
401 LAFAYETTE STREET
NEW YORK, NEW YORK 10003

PRINTED IN THE UNITED STATES OF AMERICA
BY HADDON CRAFTSMEN, SCRANTON, PENNSYLVANIA

For Arnold and Jennifer,
Joseph and my mother,
and in loving memory of my father

A special thanks to all the people at Eureka Florist, and to the North Coast Writers, particularly my writing partner, Emma. I'd also like to thank my sister, Mary Shumate, for her help.

Chapter One

*A*lison Simmons arched her back and rolled her shoulders as she stuck a glorious red rosebud into a vase already greened with Ming fern. If she had a penny for every dozen roses that had passed through Two Hearts Florist this Valentine's Day, she'd have—

"Ali?" Deanne said.

Seventy-eight cents, Alison decided. Seventy-eight dozen pink, white, yellow, lavender, peach, orange, and red roses.

This time Deanne's voice was a trifle more insistent. "Earth to boss lady . . . come in, please."

"What? Oh, sorry, Deanne. Just thinking."

"What about?" Deanne asked as she glanced at her watch.

Alison put in the last rose and reached for the baby's breath. She shrugged, unwilling to admit to Deanne, who had been covering for her for the better part of two months, how stiff and sore she really was.

"Just a little tired," she said lightly.

"I bet you miss Jamie too, don't you?" Deanne asked, concern flickering across her face.

Jamie. Alison smiled and nodded and didn't know how to answer. Yes, she did, a lot . . . and yet, no. The mere thought that she could feel that ambiguous about a six-year-old child, a child who was now her responsibility, was upsetting in itself.

"Well, I think you're great," Deanne said. "I mean, there you were six weeks ago, minding your own sweet business, when wham, all of a sudden a cousin you hardly know dies and leaves you a ton of money, her kid, a huge old house, and that sourpuss of a lawyer, Mr. Morton."

"Mr. Morgan," Alison corrected automatically. She'd never thought about it that way before. No wonder she sometimes felt like a piece of driftwood buffeted by conflicting tides.

"Whatever. I just know it hasn't been easy for you." Deanne went back to arranging neon-yellow tulips as she added, "Jamie will be better off with you than he was with his own mother."

"Deanne, please."

"Oh, I know, my mouth is too big." She

rested both hands on the counter and leaned forward. "But I mean it, Ali. Okay, okay, I can see I'm embarrassing you."

"Thanks, anyway," Alison said.

Deanne grinned. "No problem. Besides, I want something."

"I should have guessed—"

"I need to get out of here." Deanne finished off the tulips by spritzing them with liquid preservative, inserted a card pick, and looked at Alison. "How about it?"

"You and Ben have a big evening planned?"

Deanne grinned. "Yep. Hate leaving you in the lurch, but Chris is out front soothing the frenzied masses, and it *is* past seven. I'm meeting Ben at the restaurant, and the reservations are for twenty minutes from now."

Alison kicked off one shoe and rubbed the bare arch on the top of her other foot. "Then you'd better hurry. Go on, I can finish up here. And say hello to that husband of yours."

Deanne exchanged her smock for her coat, buttoning the latter against the damp Northern California evening. She bit at her lower lip before venturing a question. "Would this be a good time to ask if there were any takers on your ad?"

"Which ad? The one for a baby-sitter or the one for a flower designer?" Alison laughed wryly and added, "Don't bother answering— it doesn't matter. I haven't found anyone for anything."

"There's that worried look again," Deanne said. "I've seen it scamper across your face a dozen times today. Why don't you take tomorrow morning off? You look a little beat."

"Okay," Alison agreed readily. She'd promised Jamie a walk—as if he'd hold her to it.

Chris stuck her head in the door that led to the front. "I need a single red rose," she said. "Are those two arrangements ready?"

Alison waved a hand. "Take them."

Deanne escaped out the back door while Alison selected one of the last red roses, inserted its stem into a water tube, and wrapped it and a delicate branch of baby's breath in tissue. Some lucky someone was going to receive a token, a lover's pledge, she told herself, and it had to look as picture perfect as the first rose she'd wrapped that morning. Chris arrived back to collect the rose, her freckled cheeks flushed with haste. She handed Alison a new order and asked if they were out of orchids.

"We have a few left. What do you need?"

"Three white ones arranged in this." She handed Alison a fragile crystal bowl, then dug another order out of her pocket and slapped it down on the counter. "That's for a dozen purple roses, delivered to this address by nine."

Alison took the phalaenopsis orchids from the walk-in refrigerator and briefly admired their exotic beauty. All she'd wanted, since she was tall enough to see over the counter, was to own this shop and make it special. Four years of hard work had marked the beginning of a transformation, but she needed more time, and now time was something she had precious little of. Jamie needed time too, and, of course, he was a lot more important than a store.

"Ali? There's someone here to see you," Chris said. She lowered her voice and added, "A real hunk."

Alison inserted the last orchid and deftly tied a raspberry ribbon to insert amid the greens. "To see me? What does he want?" She handed Chris the orchids. "Five more to go, all deliveries."

"Ooh, this is pretty. The hunk's here about the ad."

Alison took a deep breath as she pushed her hair off her forehead and thought. A male flower designer? Great! There hadn't been a man around since her father had turned over the keys four years before on her twentieth birthday.

"Might as well send him in. We'll give him

a trial by fire. Are there any more customers out there?"

"Just the guy for these orchids. All the others bought flowers out of the display case." Chris glanced at her watch. "It's almost seven-thirty. Shall I lock the door?"

Alison looked around the workroom. The floor was littered with flower stems and scraps of ribbons, the counters covered with arrangements still to be delivered.

"Go ahead," she told Chris. "Do you mind closing out the cash register and then helping me clean up this mess and loading the van?"

"Sure." Chris shook her head and added, "You shouldn't have taken so many late orders this afternoon."

"Probably not," Alison agreed as she put a long white box on the worktable, but she was glad she had. The best part of owning a florist shop was helping people express themselves. Some people just weren't as organized as others. Besides, the personal touch, the willingness to work a little harder and longer, was helping her revive a business her dad had let grow stale.

She lined the box with tissue and fern and selected twelve pale lavender roses, vaguely aware of Chris's voice, the ring of the cash register, then the bell on the door.

"Hello," a male voice said.

Alison looked up, startled. He'd come in quietly. The first thing she noticed about him were the eyeglasses that perched on his straight nose. He was, indeed, attractive.

"Hello," she finally answered. "I'm Alison Simmons."

He held out his hand, which she shook. "Jack Foxx. I'm here to apply for the job."

"Of course. Well, you picked a good day." She looked through the remaining orders and chose a simple carnation in a vase. "Put this together."

"What?"

She looked up. He was holding the order form as though it might bite him. "Put it together. You know, grab one of those glass vases over there and put a carnation and some fern in it. Let's see your work."

He looked liked a cornered mouse. He wasn't the first, Alison thought as she began layering the flowers with winter bud. Everyone wanted to work in a florist shop. The trick was finding someone who both wanted to and knew how.

When she looked up again, he was still puzzling over the order form. He caught her gaze and grinned. "No problem," he said. She watched as he selected a red carnation and some asparagus fern. She wouldn't have chosen that particular fern herself as it was expensive and the order had a top price of seven dollars and fifty cents, but it did look nice. He took a tall vase from the shelf and stared at it, then at the flower as though they were two halves of some mysterious whole.

"There's a pail of water already mixed with preservative right by your feet," she told him.

"Good," he said, nodding. He filled the vase, stuck in the flower, stuck in the fern, and looked back at her.

"Pretty good, huh?"

She shook her head. "The flower is tilted, and you didn't cut the stem." She handed him a spool of thin white ribbon printed with tiny red hearts and added, "Jazz it up a little."

He started unrolling ribbon as Alison put the lid on the box of roses and tied a huge plum-colored bow around it, tucking in the card that had been filled out earlier. Then she looked back at Jack. He was elbow deep in ribbon.

"You don't even know how to tie a bow, do you?" she asked. She was disappointed because he'd seemed like a competent man, not the kind to apply for a job he wasn't qualified for. Besides, once she'd looked past the glasses, she'd found deep-brown eyes and an intriguing smile that played across his lips from time to time. "I can't believe you're an experienced floral designer," she told him. "What do you really do?"

He gave up on the ribbon and looked at her sheepishly. "I teach comparative literature at Humboldt University," he said, naming a school less then ten miles away. "I'm on a year's leave of absence right now."

Alison narrowed her eyes. "So you decided to fulfill a lifetime desire to work in a florist shop?"

"Not exactly," he said. "I believe you met my grandmother last week. Samantha Askarian—remember her? Sweet little old thing with an inner core of molten lava?"

Alison shook her head. "I'm sorry—"

"It wasn't here," he interrupted. "It was at your house. She was applying for a job as a nanny for your cousin's son."

"Of course, I remember her." She did too. Mrs. Askarian was perfect for the job of Jamie's nanny except that she was allergic to dogs. Unfortunately, Jamie's best friend was a seventy-pound golden Labrador named Nora.

"Anyway," Jack concluded, "that's the job I'm here to apply for."

"Nanny? You?"

"Well, of course," he said, looking down at

the listing carnation. "Unless you think I show a latent talent for floral design."

"No. I mean—"

"I can see I've thrown you for a loop," he interrupted. "I saw your ad in the newspaper this morning, so I knew you hadn't found anyone yet. When I called the house, I got the cook."

"Mrs. Potter."

"That's right. She said you weren't home, that I might be able to find you here."

"Which explains how you got here but not why a college professor would apply for a job as a six-year-old's nanny," Alison said as she snatched another order form and started gathering the flowers.

Jack leaned forward, resting both his elbows on the workbench across from her. He looked totally at ease in his leather jacket and white shirt, as though he hung around the back room of florist shops all the time.

"It's not as nutty as it sounds," he began. "As I said, I'm not teaching right now. Moved home to help Gram out when Grandfather died—thought she'd need a male shoulder to lean on. I was wrong about that, by the way. Gram is looking for a part-time job, and I'm underfoot. My apartment is sublet till fall, so

I thought working for you, baby-sitting Jamie, would be the perfect solution."

Alison quickly cut a small piece of green oasis and fit it into a heart-shaped mug, taping it securely, her hands moving automatically as she considered his words. Choosing a stem of pink mini carnations, she asked, "What are your qualifications? What makes you think you'd be a decent baby-sitter for a six-year-old child who lost his mother a few short weeks ago?"

"Well, let's see. I'm a thirty-year-old kid at heart, the oldest of three boys, taught sailing at a summer camp for six- to eight-year-olds for four summers during college, have two little nephews who think I'm wonderful, and I like kids." He grinned as he added, "Oh, and I'm not allergic to dogs."

"It's not that simple," Alison said, wondering how to explain. Mavis and she had never been close. The eighteen-year age difference, to say nothing of their own mothers' lack of interest in each other, meant they seldom met. Besides, Alison had spent her youth hanging around the shop to learn the business. She gathered Mavis's sole interest in flowers had been receiving them from ardent admirers.

And now, thanks to a terrible automobile accident that had claimed Mavis while she was vacationing in Europe, Alison had Jamie. To be exact, just as Deanne had said earlier, she had Jamie, a huge house, money, a staff, and problems she previously hadn't known existed, number one being Jamie himself. He was a shy, quiet little boy who really didn't know her and, quite honestly, gave no indication he ever wanted to.

"Jamie needs understanding," she said slowly. "He's small for his age, and he's been sheltered. Miss Hall, his counselor, says his life shouldn't be disrupted for two years. Mr. Morgan, Mavis's . . . my lawyer, believes he belongs in a boarding school. I just want someone sensitive to look after him." She snapped a carnation stem as she silently chided herself for telling this stranger so much. He was easy to talk to, though.

Jack leaned closer. "I can be very sensitive," he said.

"Yes. Well, I'm not doubting that, but I don't think a man would be the best thing. I know that sounds sexist, and I apologize, but Jamie isn't used to men."

"His mother never had men around?"

She felt her cheeks grow warm—one of the curses of being a blue-eyed blonde—as she thought of the swarms of men Mavis had surrounded herself with. First, she'd married money, divorced it, married it again, then been widowed. Jamie came as an afterthought. His father, a generation older than Mavis, had died before Jamie was even born. After that, there'd been men to travel with, men to dance with, men to party with. But no men for Jamie, at least none Alison knew of.

"Just the men she dated," Alison mumbled. After all, Mavis was her cousin, and she wasn't going to discuss any shortcomings with Jack Foxx. "So, I'm sure you can see that he needs a woman who—"

"Listen," Jack interrupted, "let's get real here. How hard can looking after one little kid be?"

Alison smiled slowly. Hadn't she thought the same thing herself? Well, he'd never know because she had no intention of hiring him.

Misreading her silence, Jack added, "You won't even know he's around."

"You don't understand at all," she said firmly. "I want to be part of his life."

He twirled a piece of fern in his fingers and raised his eyebrows.

"I mean it," she insisted. "Jamie and I just need time to—well, to get to know each other." She hoped with all her heart that this was true.

"I'm sorry," he said immediately. "I didn't mean to offend you." He looked at her thoughtfully for a few seconds, assessing something. At last he said, "Gram came home from her interview kind of upset. She told me how your cook took it upon herself to fire Jamie's latest nanny as soon as his mother died. Gram liked Jamie, but she didn't think much of that lawyer you lean on, and she was worried about your lack of experience."

"Your grandmother is quite opinionated," Alison muttered, annoyed. She hardly needed to be reminded that she lacked experience. As for leaning on Mr. Morgan, well, suppose she did now and then? Big deal.

Jack laughed softly. "I warned you Gram's comfortable exterior hid steel. She wasn't being cruel, though. She just loves children. She told me you were having a hard time finding the right nanny, so presto, here I am."

"Ah, your grandmother sent you."

"Nope. This is my idea. Hey, I don't get paid when I don't teach. I need a job, and I think maybe it would be nice for your nephew to have a man around for a while." He reached into his inside jacket pocket and took out a folded sheet of paper. "Here are my references. At least look at them, Alison."

She took the paper but didn't unfold it.

"Give me a try," he coaxed. "I'd like to meet the boy."

"You'd get bored stiff in a week and want to leave," she said. "Jamie doesn't need that kind of turmoil after what he's been through."

Jack stared at her for a second, as though sorting his thoughts. She thought she saw a frown crease his forehead, and the suspicion surfaced in her mind that he wasn't being completely up-front.

"I have a . . . project . . ." he said slowly. "I'd work on that while Jamie was in school and after he went to bed. Believe me, I won't be bored."

This time Alison stared. "Hmm—" she said, but despite her misgivings Jack's hesitation before and after the word "project" intrigued her.

"Jamie would always come first," Jack pledged with a mock salute.

She met his gaze and reluctantly smiled. There was something so irreverent about the man, so refreshing after the cook's dour attitude and Jamie's silence.

"I can't think," she told him, even though common sense said there was nothing to think about. "My head hurts, my feet hurt, and I'm tired. Mr. Morgan—you remember him, he's the lawyer I lean on—is coming to dinner tomorrow night about seven. Why don't you come too? If he thinks it's a good idea, then we'll see."

Jack straightened up to his whole six feet. "Okay."

"No promises," she added quickly. "Understood?"

"Understood," he said. "And thanks. Shall I let myself out the back door?"

"Please," she said and watched as he left. "I must be nuts," she said aloud.

None of the flowers shook their petaled heads in disagreement.

Chapter Two

*A*lison was up early the next morning. It was Saturday, so Jamie would be home. She pulled on a pair of jeans and a sweater, then looked into his room to see if he was awake. His bed was rumpled—and empty.

Grace, the part-time housekeeper who had come with the house along with Mrs. Potter and the furniture, was in the den. She flung her feather duster with carefree abandon until she saw Alison.

"Good morning. Do you know where Jamie is?" Alison asked.

"He's in the kitchen with the cook, miss," Grace said and went back to dusting, turning her back on Alison, not wanting or expecting thanks. Alison honestly didn't think she'd ever get used to people expecting her to treat them like servants.

The kitchen was easily as big as any room

in the old Victorian house, a gleaming tribute to a mixture of modern and old-fashioned. Representing the modern aspect were two microwaves, some kind of fancy Formica countertops, and a stove as big as a twin bed. The old-fashioned aspect was represented by oak walls, black-and-white-checkered tile floors, an open-beam pine ceiling, and a compact, cast-iron fireplace. Behind the fireplace a narrow door led to the basement. A small round table occupied the center of the room, while winter sunlight streamed through the back door where Nora faithfully leaned against the glass, looking in, keeping both golden eyes glued to Jamie.

Jamie said, "No!" It was obviously not the first time he'd said it.

"You will, and that's that!" Mrs. Potter snarled behind his shoulder.

Physically Jamie resembled his slightly built, dark-eyed father, but Alison was beginning to suspect he'd inherited his red-haired, green-eyed mother's stubborn streak.

"Is there a problem?" she asked as she poured herself a cup of coffee.

Both the cook and Jamie glowered at her. Neither answered.

"Maybe you guys need an impartial arbitrator," she added. "You know, like a labor/management negotiator. I volunteer."

Her gaze followed Jamie's to the plate in front of him. It was a picture suitable for a gourmet magazine: eggs Benedict awash in hollandaise sauce, sliced kiwi fruit, a bowl of out-of-season raspberries peeping through a thick blanket of cream, and a glass of what appeared to be freshly squeezed grapefruit juice.

"He won't eat," Mrs. Potter announced, "and he's in a snit because I won't allow that beast Nora into the house."

Nora, the beast in question, heard her name. She sat up straight and thumped her tail against the glass. Her yellow fur was muddy and damp.

"Nora's a mess," Alison told Jamie. "We'll brush her later. Meanwhile, don't you want this beautiful breakfast Mrs. Potter was kind enough to fix you?" She put a hand out to touch him but stopped when he looked directly at her and frowned.

"No," he announced. "I want Space Chunks."

"Sugar cereal," Mrs. Potter explained. "I won't have that junk in this house." She was a small woman with steel-gray hair, blunt features, and a tight voice. For some reason her face always looked pinched to Alison, as though something didn't smell quite right somewhere.

"Maybe there's a compromise," Alison said slowly, feeling her way over quicksand. "Let's see—do we have any healthy cold cereal in the house, Mrs. Potter?"

The cook looked as if she'd happily climb across the table and strangle her, but Alison stood her ground. It was perfectly clear Mrs. Potter was used to calling the shots, all the shots, in the house. Maybe Mavis had abdicated her parental rights to Mrs. Potter; Alison wasn't going to. It was ridiculous to expect a small boy to eat food like this.

"There's a box of shredded wheat," Mrs. Potter conceded after a lengthy pause.

"How about it, Jamie?"

Jamie seemed to weigh his options. "Okay," he said at last.

Mrs. Potter disappeared into the walk-in pantry. Her face was more pinched than ever as she set the cereal box, milk, bowl, and spoon on the table.

"And what am I supposed to do with this perfectly fine food?" she snarled.

Alison took the plate from in front of Jamie. She sat down, took a mouthful, chewed, and swallowed. The eggs were cold and congealed and sat in her stomach like a lump of modeling clay. "Delicious," she announced.

Mrs. Potter grumbled something unintelligible. Jamie poured his cereal, then set the box down between Alison and himself.

After a long walk with Jamie that was relieved from strained silence only when Nora chased a neighbor's cat up a tree and Jamie ran after her, yelling, Alison found it a relief to go to work that afternoon. It meant Mrs. Potter would take Jamie downtown for a new pair of shoes, but he'd been suffering the woman's full-time attention for weeks as it was.

"Chris told me about the hunk," Deanne said as soon as Alison divested herself of her coat. She was about the same age as Alison, but taller than her five-foot-five boss. She wore her black hair in a tangle of loose waves.

"He *is* attractive," Alison agreed.

"Come on, Ali. Did you hire him?"

"He wasn't applying for a job here. Get this—he wants to baby-sit Jamie."

Deanne threw back her head and laughed. "Wonderful!"

"I didn't hire him," Alison added hastily. She explained the situation, admitting that asking him to dinner had been a ploy to gain time to think clearly. "I can't hire him," she concluded.

"Why not? For heaven's sake, girl! I swear, the only way we're going to get you married off is to a daffodil."

"Thanks. I'm not even going to remind you that I'm looking for a baby-sitter, not a boyfriend. Enough about this, okay?" She picked up a stack of phone orders. "Anything interesting happen around here this morning?"

Deanne's expressive face lit up. "Good news and bad news. Which do you want first?"

"The bad," Alison said with a sigh.

"Oh. Well, everyone's favorite landlord, Herman Singleton himself, called on us this morning."

"I take it he didn't want flowers."

"Quite the contrary. He had Chris wrap up a gorgeous bundle of snapdragons, I think to assuage his conscience, then he informed us he's selling the building."

Alison was looking at a floral order for the new mother of girl triplets. It took a couple of moments for Deanne's words to sink in. When they did, she felt her jaw drop. "He *what?*" she screeched.

A customer looked over. Deanne pushed Alison into the back room. "Your lease is almost up," she reminded her.

"But he always renews the lease."

"This time he's got a buyer for the building."

"I can't believe this," Alison groaned. When Mavis died and Alison found out how much money she'd inherited, she toyed with the idea of buying the building, but abandoned it. It just didn't feel right to use Mavis's money on her business. She knew the major reason she'd been named in the will was so that she'd be wealthy enough to provide Mavis's idea of a decent life for Jamie.

"Can't you buy the building?" Deanne asked.

"Maybe," Alison said uncertainly.

"He's going to call you at home over the weekend."

"Okay. Gives me some time to think. What's the good news?"

"We booked a wedding. Mother of the bride came in herself. Don't get too excited, though, because I predict she's going to be a pain in the neck! Insisted on talking to the owner—to you, for instance. She'd hardly give me the time of day."

"That's silly," Alison agreed.

"Tell Mrs. Howell."

The name rang a bell. "Courtney Howell's mother?"

"Yeah. You know her?"

"No," Alison said, but she thought she remembered where she'd seen the daughter's name recently. "Do we have a newspaper here?"

Deanne fetched the paper; then Alison flipped through to the society page. There it was in two-inch bold-face type: LOCAL SOCIALITE TO WED BARTON FIELDING. Courtney Howell's picture smiled up from the printed page atop a three-column story that began, *The daughter of prominent businessman Daniel Horatio Howell and the son of Texas oil magnate "Hack" Fielding announced their engagement yesterday at a lavish party in the Howell home. . . .*

"Where do you suppose she heard about us?" Deanne mused.

"I have no idea," Alison admitted, but her heart was beating faster. A big wedding done well would mean other big weddings. It could be a stepping-stone to making Two Hearts Florist a success. If there was a Two Hearts Florist after Mr. Singleton got finished with them.

"You've got a dreamy look in your eyes," Deanne said, laughing.

"We'll buy this building and expand," Alison predicted. "This is just the beginning, Deanne—you watch."

They grinned at each other and went about

the afternoon orders with a renewed sense of joy. Alison couldn't help wondering why the Howells had chosen Two Hearts when there were other, better-known, larger shops in town, but she wasn't going to question fate. Besides, Deanne had arranged for mother and daughter to come in Monday afternoon, and she could ask them then.

The shop wasn't far from Mavis's house. Alison left the van at the shop for Chris to make the late deliveries and walked the eight blocks home. She left a little early to be sure to have time to prepare for her guests. Not that she had all that much to do. Mrs. Potter did all the cooking, Grace cleaned, after a fashion, and Jamie usually played in his room.

She pulled her coat around herself as she walked the uncrowded sidewalk. After the two years Jamie's counselor recommended had passed, they could move to a smaller place. She missed doing things for herself even if her idea of cooking was sticking a frozen pizza into the microwave. Besides, she didn't feel they needed all that space and all those people.

The house sat on one square block of prime city land, two-thirds surrounded with a five-foot-high white-brick fence. Alison let herself in the gate and took the brick walk up to the house. Instead of going up the broad steps to the front door, she followed the path to the left, around the side.

A huge magnolia tree spread like a canopy above her head. A separate entrance to a basement as big as the whole ground floor of the house descended off to the right. In back was a willow tree and a pond, where she could see Nora snuffling in the grass.

She let herself in the French doors of the den and collapsed on the leather swivel chair that sat thronelike behind a desk as big as a subcompact car. The rest of the room was done tastefully in a deep aqua and peach, the furniture polished cherry, the ceiling-high shelves filled with books and mementos collected by Mavis as she traveled.

"The Howell/Fielding wedding," she chuckled to herself as she swiveled the chair to look through the French doors to the pond beyond. "What a coup!" Not even the threat of what Mr. Singleton had in mind for her building could dampen her enthusiasm.

She turned when she heard the squeak of the hall door. Jamie stood in the doorway, all elbows and ears, his eyes dark pools. Behind him stood Mrs. Potter. Alison felt the grin slide off her face as Jamie broke away from Mrs. Potter and ran across the room to her.

Chapter Three

"Pumpkin," Alison managed to squeak before Jamie threw his forty some-odd pounds into her lap. The little boy buried his head in Alison's hair. She could feel his small body shake with quiet sobs. She stroked the back of his head, her gaze searching Mrs. Potter's pale face for a clue. The older woman just looked mad.

"Mrs. Potter?" she said at last. "What in the world is wrong with Jamie?"

"What you see there is nothing more than a tantrum, Miss Simmons—plain and clear, a tantrum. Jamie wanted those canvas shoes. You know very good and well that his mother always insisted on buying him brown leather oxfords of the very best quality. He's throwing a tantrum because I wouldn't get him what he wants. Maybe it's not my place to say it, but

27

you're condoning his fit by comforting him like that."

"I'm not condoning anything," Alison said over the child's soft cries. "Shh, honey. Let's get to the bottom of this, okay?" She finally managed to peel him from her chest where he had clung like a limpet. He wiped at his eyes with the backs of his fists and hiccupped.

"Now you've done it," she teased. "Now you've got the hiccups. Mrs. Potter, will you please get Jamie a glass of water?" She tried to ignore the glare Mrs. Potter threw her way before stomping from the room, but it was hard. Alison felt as though she were back in the quicksand, her instincts telling her a small boy wanting some sneakers instead of leather oxfords was hardly surprising. Why hadn't Mrs. Potter just gotten the boy what he wanted? Why did it matter?

She looked down at Jamie's feet. He was still wearing his old brown shoes. They were ugly. Jamie was looking into her eyes when she glanced back at him. He had such black, bottomless eyes. He hiccupped.

"You don't like these shoes much, do you?" Alison asked.

He shook his head. Now that the crisis was over, he was distancing himself again. She wanted to grab him back but made her hands

lie still on his legs. His gray slacks were as spot-
less as his white shirt. It occurred to Alison for
the hundredth time that he looked like a child
from the fifties, not the eighties. Why had
Mavis dressed him like this?

Mrs. Potter returned with the water. "I can
take him again Monday afternoon," she said
as she put the water down in front of Jamie.

Jamie hiccupped but hesitated taking the
glass. Alison didn't much blame him as she,
too, was finding it hard to swallow with Mrs.
Potter's disapproving stare blanketing them
both.

She picked up the glass and put it into
Jamie's hands. "Little swallows," she cau-
tioned, then looked at Mrs. Potter. "Thanks,
anyway, Mrs. Potter, but I think I'll take
Jamie. I agree that he shouldn't have thrown
a tantrum like that, though considering everything, I suppose we have to expect a few minor
behavior problems." Mrs. Potter looked un-
moved. For heaven's sake, Alison thought, did
she have to come right out and yell, "Give the
kid a break!"?

"Anyway," she continued, "I'll pick him up
after school Monday and take him shoe shopping. Maybe some Nikes would be just the
thing for spring."

"It's winter," Mrs. Potter pointed out. "His mother always insisted on oxfords."

I'm his mother now, Alison thought, but she didn't say it. "Almost spring. We'll fudge a little."

Mrs. Potter dug in her heels. "Miss Simmons, I have been in charge of dressing Jamie since he was born. Mrs. Dufour trusted my judgment implicitly. I know my job title is cook, but—"

"Some things are bound to change," Alison interrupted softly. She tried to choose her words carefully because in between hiccups and swallows of water, Jamie was listening. "I'd just like to get him some Nikes."

Mrs. Potter planted her hands on her waist. She riveted her eyes on Alison. "I was going to wait for a while, Miss Simmons, but perhaps it would be better for all concerned if I did it now." She paused.

Alison took the opportunity to send Jamie upstairs. There was something very ominous about the set of Mrs. Potter's jaw.

"Now, as I was saying," Mrs. Potter continued once Jamie disappeared through the door. "All things considered, I have decided to seek employment elsewhere."

Alison didn't know whether to greet the news with a hoot of laughter or a shower of tears. Mrs. Potter was quitting! How many times had she thought of firing the woman but had been unable to bring herself to do it? As few upheavals as possible, Jamie's counselor had warned, and she'd taken the advice literally.

"I assure you, I am serious," Mrs. Potter warned. "Mrs. Dufour was a lovely woman. She didn't have too much time for the little boy, and the nannies she hired were so unsuitable that I took it upon myself to manage the child's life. In the last month you have consistently interfered with my decisions."

Alison thrust herself out of the chair and strode toward the hall door. Unsure of what to say, she said nothing. She was unsure how Mrs. Potter's leaving would affect Jamie.

"I've already found another job," Mrs. Potter announced smugly. Her gaze followed Alison as she paced around the den. "I was going to start next month, but they are very anxious to have me. I want to leave right away."

Alison stopped pacing. "Right away? As in when?"

"As soon as possible."

"You may leave whenever you want, of course," Alison said stiffly, "but I wish you would consider Jamie. As for my stepping on your toes, I really don't see how—"

Mrs. Potter recited, "You let him eat peanut butter and jelly, play with his toys downstairs, have Nora in the house, run about without his slippers. . . . Do you see what I mean? I simply can't live here like this. Besides, you hardly eat anything, and you never entertain. I don't have enough to do."

Alison decided not to point out that with Mavis dead less than two months, it hardly seemed proper to entertain in her home. Anyway, it wouldn't have mattered if it had been two years. She just wasn't the entertaining type. Her idea of a party was Deanne, Ben, Sam, Chris, and take-out Chinese food.

But it was more than this that quelled her tongue. She was finally getting a picture of life in this opulent house. Jamie upstairs, Mavis gone or partying, Mrs. Potter juggling them both, suffering some poor nanny's occasional interference. Things were different now, thank goodness.

"I guess you have to do what you have to do," Alison said.

"Yes," Mrs. Potter agreed. "I know Mr. Morgan is expected for dinner, so I'll stay through tonight."

"There's no need," Alison replied, as eager now to be rid of Mrs. Potter as Mrs. Potter was to be rid of her. "I will take care of dinner my-self."

Mrs. Potter's lip curled in what Alison took to be a sneer. She nodded curtly and left the room.

Honestly! Alison tore open the French doors and slammed them behind her, determined to put as much distance between herself and that woman as she could.

The grass needed mowing. It was damp enough to stain her suede shoes, but she didn't care. She stalked through it toward the pond, taking big, deep gulps of fresh air. A slight breeze had come up. Daffodils greeted her with a toss of their heavy heads.

Nora appeared from nowhere, her feet muddy and her mouth open with what looked like a smile. The big golden dog lumbered up and stuck her muzzle into Alison's hand.

"Good dog," Alison told her. "Boy, are you a mess!"

Nora panted happily. No wonder Jamie was so crazy about the dog. Alison had always found her presence here a little disconcerting. Mavis seemed the Yorkshire terrier type, but here was Nora, seventy pounds of hair, dirt, and smell—totally dog. At least Cousin Mavis had thought of Jamie when she bought a dog. Alison brushed away a tear from her cheek, unsure if it was for Mavis or Jamie or both of them.

The pond was small and shallow and half covered with water hyacinths. She stomped around it, feeling her nerves unwind as her muscles flexed. She broke off a twig of curly willow, noting the tree could use a good pruning. She put it on her mental list of things to do, right behind finding a new designer for the shop, a new cook for the house, and a baby-sitter for Jamie.

Good grief, What's-his-name was coming to dinner! What was his name? Her anger with Mrs. Potter had completely driven it from her mind. Oh, well, he could take potluck along with everyone else. That should kill any lurking desire he had to live in this house and baby-sit a six-year-old. What a crazy idea!

She took off to circumnavigate the fenced yard, Nora alongside, but her mind was focused on What's-his-name. What in the world would a college professor want with a menial job like this? The man probably thought he could laze around working on his "project" while Jamie played quietly in the other room and she wrote him weekly checks.

And what exactly was this project he was so mysterious about? Was he hiding something? It irritated her that he presented himself as an expert. What had he said—something like, "How hard can looking after one little kid be?" And he called *her* inexperienced?

"Jack Foxx, that's his name," she told Nora, who took the twig of curly willow from her hand and crunched it in two.

By now she'd made it to the front of the house. The sun hovered low in the sky. She glanced at her watch and was surprised to see it was after five.

As Alison turned to go back into the house, the sun caught and splintered on the upstairs windows. It really was a lovely house. Four stories—if you counted the basement room—of one-hundred-year-old splendor, covered with bric-a-brac and gingerbread, softened with dove-gray paint and white trim. White camellia trees stood on either side of the brick walk, wisteria vines climbed the pillars framing the front door, and tulips and irises dotted the yard, their natural-looking clusters belying a gardener's hand.

Grace's beat-up old Ford was parked beside the garage, which was placed at an angle and open to the street and the curved front drive. Mavis's white Mercedes was still parked in the garage, though Mr. Morgan had hinted he wanted to buy it. Mrs. Potter didn't drive, preferring taxis. Alison drove her van, complete with multithousands of miles on the odometer. It was hers. She'd bought it herself and had had it painted pink. An intricate design of dogwood blossoms and vines decorated the sides and circled the words *Two Hearts Florist.* When she got a little more money, she planned on buying a second van.

A little more money. She stopped walking. She could buy a fleet of pink vans if she wanted! Why did it bother her so much to think of using Mavis's money on her shop?

"Because the shop is mine," she told Nora, and the dog looked at her as though it made perfect sense. "I'll use Mavis's money to support Jamie and this mausoleum as long as I have to, but I won't let it change my life." Nora panted in agreement. "Anyone ever tell you that you're a dandy little listener?" she added. Nora wagged her whole rear end.

Alison opened the front door with her key, leaving Nora, dirtier now than ever, on the front porch. The entry was the same checkered black-and-white tile as the kitchen. Off to the left were the double doors that led into the den. To the right was the living room where Mavis used to amuse her friends by playing the piano and singing. The dining room, kitchen, and servants' quarters were beyond the living room, a TV room and guest suite beyond the den.

In the middle of the entry was an oak staircase, carpeted in a deep peach-colored plush. At the top of the stairs was an open balcony with six bedrooms and baths leading from it, and beyond them, stairs that led to the little-used third floor. Nothing was missing. Nothing one could actually see, anyway.

Mrs. Potter appeared on the balcony. Her rooms were on the ground floor, so she must have been in saying good-bye to Jamie. Alison wondered if he was upset.

Mrs. Potter came purposefully down the stairs. Alison kept her head high.

"I've told Jamie," Mrs. Potter said. "I'm ready to go."

"If you must," Alison said. "Would you like me to drive you to your new job or call a cab for you?"

"I've already called one," Mrs. Potter said. If the woman felt any sadness at leaving her home of four years, Alison couldn't see it.

A brief honk sounded from outside. Alison opened the front door and waved to the taxi driver, who was busy talking to Nora.

"Please tell him to drive along to the kitchen entrance," Mrs. Potter said. "My things are out there."

Alison imparted this news. Mrs. Potter pulled on her gloves, opened her mouth as if to say something, then closed it.

"I'll write a check for your last month's wages," Alison said formally.

"No need. I've left my new address on the pad by the kitchen phone. Just have Mr. Morgan settle my wages."

They nodded at each other. Then Mrs. Potter turned and walked toward the kitchen, her low heels making crisp little clicking sounds on the tile. Seconds later Alison heard the kitchen door close and the taxi take off down the drive.

She started to sigh but stopped when she caught sight of Grace peering out from the dining room. She was about thirty, quiet, and seemed to be involved in an on-and-off-again marriage. She wore her mousy brown hair in a low bun that rested on her neck. Alison had never seen her wear anything but a black jumper and white blouse, clothes that looked too big and did nothing to flatter her sallow skin. Alison smiled as she stepped forward.

"Is Potter gone?" Grace asked. "I mean, gone for good?"

Alison nodded. "She quit."

Grace narrowed her eyes. It was hard for Alison to read her expression. What if Grace decided to follow suit and quit too? *If she does,*

Alison thought rebelliously, *I'll take Jamie and move into a tent.*

"I could come extra days," Grace said. "I wouldn't mind."

"You wouldn't? Can you cook?"

Grace scrunched up her mouth and nose. "Sorry, miss. I open cans."

"Me too," Alison confessed. She'd always been too busy watching Dad and Grandma arrange flowers to watch Mom cook. "Listen, Grace. I would like it if you came more often, every day if you're up to it. But please, please call me Alison. Jamie is Jamie; you are Grace."

Grace smiled broadly. "Okay. But Danny works split shift. I have to be home by four o'clock, five the latest."

"Fine. You'd better get going, then. It's almost five-thirty."

"I'll come tomorrow," Grace promised.

"Tomorrow is Sunday," Alison reminded her.

She shrugged. "Danny sleeps most of the day. I'll come."

"Fine." Alison started up the stairs to find out how Jamie was taking Mrs. Potter's mutiny, but paused to turn when Grace called her name.

"I never did like that woman," Grace said softly.

Alison laughed and continued up the stairs.

Chapter Four

Jamie seemed fine, his hiccups gone, his attention focused on three small metal cars. He'd pushed back the wool oriental carpet and was intent on racing miniature cars across the hardwood floor. He barely looked up when Alison entered, didn't bat an eye when she told him Mrs. Potter wasn't coming back.

"Want to help me fix dinner?" she asked.

To her surprise Jamie looked up. For a second Alison thought she saw pleasure on his small face, but it was gone in a blink. "I don't know how to cook," he said sullenly.

"I don't, either," she admitted. "I'll take any help I can get."

Jamie slowly got to his feet. He stuffed a car or two into his pockets and followed her down the stairs.

"What are we going to cook?" he asked.

As far as Alison knew, the only things he

41

liked were peanut-butter-and-jelly sandwiches and Space Chunks cereal. She could hardly serve either one of those.

"We're having guests," she told him as she opened the refrigerator. "Mr. Morgan is coming and a man named Jack Foxx."

Jamie said, "Oh." He ducked beneath her arm and peered into the refrigerator with her. The top of his head brushed the underside of her arm. She wanted to wrap him in a big hug but didn't dare.

The dominant occupant of the top shelf was a prime-rib roast, obviously Mrs. Potter's choice for company dinner. Alison closed the fridge. There wasn't time to cook a roast, even if she knew how. There might be time to microwave it, but the only things she'd "zapped" were instant soup, popcorn, and, of course, pizza. A roast was way out of her league.

"Where do you guys keep canned food?" she asked Jamie. "You know, tomato soup, chili, ravioli, things like that?"

He shrugged his thin shoulders, as much a foreigner in the kitchen as she was. They began opening cupboards. In the end, when she finally found the canned foods, there was nothing more than button mushrooms, kumquat slices, tomato sauce, and pickled beets. Alison was in the land of fresh squeezed, fresh baked, fresh bought. These people did not eat the same way she did, or rather, had.

"What are we going to eat?" Jamie asked.

"I don't know," Alison admitted. Back to the fridge. She picked up the roast. "How long do you suppose you have to cook one of these things?" she asked Jamie.

He shrugged. "Can't we have peanut butter, Cousin Alison?"

She looked at her watch, then back at him. "Why not? You find the jelly. I'll make toasted cheese sandwiches too. Is that celery? Good. Let's get to it, Jamie."

"I get to cook?" he asked, wide-eyed.

"Certainly. You don't honestly think I can do it all by myself, do you?"

While Jamie pulled a chair to the sink and began scrubbing carrots for carrot strips, Alison sliced cheddar cheese. Jamie answered her plea for a loaf of bread with a blank stare, so she rummaged through the cupboards till she finally found one. It wasn't store-bought bread, however, but French bread from the bakery. It was so fresh it was difficult to slice, but smelled so good both Jamie and Alison buttered a piece and ate it as they worked.

Alison made carrot sticks while Jamie spread peanut butter and jelly on himself and, occasionally, on the bread. Then he filled celery with cream cheese while she put together toasted sandwiches.

"Looks good," Jamie said. The peanut-butter sandwiches were stacked on a beautiful Spode china platter Alison had found in the china hutch. The vegetables were in heavy lead-crystal bowls, ready to be carefully carried to the table. A soft sizzling noise announced the cheese sandwiches were cooking in an electric frying pan. Jamie had found a package of cookies and had neatly stacked them into twin towers.

"Yes, it does," she agreed. It probably looked better to Jamie than it would to Mr. Morgan, however. But it was edible and too late to cancel dinner, and she wouldn't give Mrs. Potter the satisfaction, anyway. "Put the peanut butter away," she directed, "and remind me to unplug that pan, okay? I'll go set the table."

By the time the doorbell rang at seven, Alison had changed from her jeans into a skirt, managed a variation of a French braid with her hair, applied a sweep of mascara to bring out her eyes, and along with Jamie finally found the linen to set the cherry dining table. She'd had Jamie lock Nora in the garage, put on a clean shirt, and open the front door.

"Jamie?" Mr. Morgan asked. He looked up

and smiled tentatively at Alison. She smiled back, not particularly eager to launch into an explanation of Mrs. Potter's whereabouts at that moment.

"You are looking lovely, my dear," he added politely, taking Alison's hands in his and squeezing briefly. Mr. Morgan was sliding into sixty, but he had managed to keep a full head of white hair. Or maybe he wore one terrific toupee. As usual, his thin hand clasped a briefcase handle. Alison contained a groan at the thought of the legalese she'd have to endure before the evening was over.

Mr. Morgan followed Alison into the spacious living room, pausing to inspect a painting hanging above the seldom-used fireplace. It was one Alison had brought from her apartment.

"Where's the Pino print?" Mr. Morgan said.

It had been hanging on the wall before she'd replaced it with a bucolic picture of a farm her mother had painted forty years before. "I put it in the den," she said. Actually, she'd put it in the darkest corner, where she wouldn't have to look at the three unattached heads floating in a sea of purple triangles.

Mr. Morgan sighed. Alison didn't think he was much of a modern-art lover, since he was firmly addicted to dark-gray three-piece suits, but the Pino had cost money. Big money, probably.

"There are a few papers for you to sign after dinner," he told Alison as he accepted the glass of wine she offered.

"Aren't there always?"

"I suppose it looks that way. Your cousin was heavily invested in many things, Miss Simmons, and it takes an active hand to keep all the balls in the air at once, so to speak."

"Yes," she agreed. She was used to papers. One didn't run a business without becoming involved in paper; sometimes there seemed to be more paper than flowers. But this stuff was different—bonds, annuities, stocks, portfolios, trusts. The list was endless and tedious.

Mr. Morgan handed Alison a personal check. "This is for the Mercedes," he explained. "I've long admired that car."

Alison looked at the check, then handed it back. "You've made a mistake."

His eyebrows rose comically. "But that's the price you agreed to earlier—"

"Not the price, the name," Alison told him patiently. "Make a new check out in Jamie's name and deposit it into his account."

"But Mavis left the car to you and—"

Alison caught sight of Jamie gesturing wildly behind Mr. Morgan's back. Alison rose.

"Please, just do as I ask. I want that money in his account." Mr. Morgan rose too, but by that time Jamie was gone. The doorbell rang. "Will you get that for me?" Alison asked as she darted off toward the kitchen.

She caught up with Jamie by the stove. One good whiff explained his actions.

"I forgot to unplug the pan!" Alison moaned dramatically. "Some cooks we are. You forgot to remind me."

Jamie looked up at Alison, then away, his shoulders hunched. She silently cursed herself. He wasn't used to her, and what had been meant as a joke must have sounded like an accusation to him. "We'll just scrape the bread a little. See? It's fine," she told him. "I'm sorry I blamed you for my Swiss-cheese memory, honey. It wasn't your fault; it was mine."

He nodded, but she sensed his reserve closing over him again.

"That doorbell should have been Mr. Foxx," she told him. "Will you go tell both men to come to dinner?"

Jamie shuffled off. Their brief collaboration was over, and they were back in their respective corners, eyeing each other warily. Alison sighed so deeply her toes curled.

She set the plate of cheese sandwiches on the table just as the three males came into the dining room. It was a pretty room done in peach and gray, the furniture richly dark and glowing with polish. She met Jack's gaze. He gave her a warm smile.

He had changed into a blue sports jacket and gray slacks. He looked just as good in these clothes as he had in the leather jacket.

"Welcome," she said brightly. "Please, sit over here by Jamie. I take it you've met Mr. Morgan?"

"Yes," Jack said.

"And Jamie?"

"Not properly, no." He stuck out his hand. Jamie stared at it for a minute, then shyly put his small hand in Jack's big one.

The table was a giant oval. Alison had set only one end of it so they could hear each other talk. Mr. Morgan shook out his napkin and draped it over his knee as he looked first at the food, then over his shoulder. Alison knew he was wondering where Mrs. Potter was.

Jamie took a peanut-butter sandwich from the platter. "Will you pass those around?" Alison asked as she handed the carrot bowl to Mr. Morgan.

He took the vegetables as he cleared his throat. With another glance thrown over his shoulder toward the kitchen door, he said, "I hear Mr. Foxx is applying for a job as Jamie's baby-sitter." There was a definite note of contempt in his voice.

Jamie looked up from dissecting his sandwich. "Really?"

"It hasn't been decided yet, sport," Jack said.

Alison watched Jack and Jamie exchange slow smiles, jealousy taking little potshots at her stomach. Jack took a cheese sandwich and a stick of celery. "That's right," Alison agreed. "Mr. Morgan? Would you like peanut butter and jelly or grilled cheese?"

He raised his eyebrows. "I beg your pardon?"

"Peanut butter or cheese," Jamie repeated impatiently.

Mr. Morgan met Alison's eyes. "One of each, I guess," he mumbled as he handed Alison his plate. His business demeanor returned within seconds. "I understand you're a professor. What exactly do you teach, Mr. Foxx?"

"Jack, please. I teach comparative literature. Right now I'm on a leave of absence."

"He's working on a project," Alison said. She was hoping to flush some details out into the open. Jack just nodded.

"Humph—" Mr. Morgan mumbled. He bit into the cheese sandwich, chewed, scowled, and wiped his mouth with his napkin. "I'm sure your academic credentials are impressive, but, of course, it's totally out of the question that you assume responsibility for the boy." He looked at the sandwich, decided against another bite, and put it back on his plate. "I can't see that comparing the literature of one culture to that of another qualifies you to care for a child Jamie's age."

"I suppose that's true," Jack said pleasantly.

Mr. Morgan waved a celery stalk as he added, "Good of you to be reasonable."

Alison took a bite of her sandwich and sneaked a peek at Jamie. He was watching Mr. Morgan intently, his huge eyes bright. He was leaning very slightly against Jack's right arm. Jack was eating awkwardly with his left hand, his right arm stiff, as though he were reluctant to dislodge the tentative contact between the boy and himself. Alison's jealousy dissipated for the time being and was replaced by a wave of tenderness.

"I understand Alison is Jamie's guardian," Jack said casually.

Mr. Morgan looked over his shoulder again. "That's correct, though, of course, she listens to my advice. She's inexperienced in these matters."

"How many children do you have?" Jack asked.

It was the first time Alison had seen Mr. Morgan speechless. He sputtered a bit and finally admitted he'd never married.

"And I understand that you advise she send Jamie to a boarding school."

Mr. Morgan was fully recovered. "That's right. He'd get the proper education there and be with people who know how to handle young children. Jamie will have certain, uh, responsibilities to assume in the future. It's imperative that he be prepared."

Alison peeked at Jamie again. He was pressed even closer to Jack.

"Besides," Mr. Morgan added, "the child needs proper male role models."

Jack leaned back in his chair and looked at Alison as though he were throwing her the ball and expected her to do something with it. She decided to try dribbling.

"Jack would be an excellent role model," she pointed out.

Mr. Morgan looked down at his plate, poked his sandwich with a carrot stick, and shook his head absently. "Mrs. Potter prepared dinner tonight?"

"Not exactly," Alison admitted.

"Me and her did," Jamie said.

"She and I," Jack and Alison corrected in unison.

"Jamie was in the kitchen?" Mr. Morgan exclaimed.

"Mrs. Potter quit," Alison said calmly. "Naturally, Jamie and I had to fix dinner."

"My dear girl," Mr. Morgan groaned. He rested his hands on either side of his plate. "You fired the cook? She ran this place. She took care of Jamie."

"She quit," Alison corrected.

"And I would like to take care of Jamie," Jack said. He looked at Jamie and added, "What do you think, kid? Think you and I could get along?" Jamie answered Jack with a wide grin. Jack looked back at Alison. "I'm positive I can handle this position."

"You must hire another cook immediately," Mr. Morgan grumbled, "or better yet, beg Mrs. Potter to reconsider. Give her a raise. And for goodness' sake, sell that little shop of yours. You hardly need the income. Furthermore, take my advice and send Jamie to one of the several good schools I've researched. I really don't see that you have any other choice. You haven't liked any of the women I've found for you except the one allergic to the child's dog."

"Nora," Jamie said quietly.

"And you refused to find the dog another home. You are simply out of options, Miss Simmons."

"I want Jack," Jamie said. "Can I have some cookies, Cousin Alison?"

Alison nodded and stared at Jack. He'd purposely goaded Mr. Morgan into this tirade, she could see that. He'd known all along that given the ball, eventually she'd go for a basket. He smiled at her, and she heard herself say, "If your references check out, you're hired."

"Good," Jack said. He and Jamie shook hands.

Mr. Morgan opened his mouth to speak, but Alison beat him to the punch. "Too late, Mr. Morgan, the decision is made. Why don't we go see to those papers so you'll have time to drive downtown in your new car for a proper dinner? Gentlemen, you'll excuse us?"

"Sure," Jamie said as he pulled two tiny cars from his pocket and showed them to Jack.

"Hey, kiddo, this one's a Porsche!" Alison heard Jack say as she preceded Mr. Morgan from the room.

Two hours, one splitting headache, and thirteen papers later she walked Mr. Morgan to the front door.

"I've been thinking about this Foxx fellow," Mr. Morgan said. "I'm afraid the man is approaching this as a novelty, a lark. Once he becomes mired in the tedious day-to-day care of a young child, he'll become intellectually bored here and move on. What will that do to Jamie?"

"Jamie will always have me," Alison said as she handed the lawyer the Mercedes' keys and the piece of folded paper Jack had given her the night before. "Besides, he assures me he has plenty to do on his own time. Please check his references, will you?"

"He mustn't assume his duties till I've a chance to check on these," Mr. Morgan said as he scanned the list. He whistled softly and added, "He knows all the right people." He tapped his chin with the folded paper. "I'd feel better if we knew why he took this leave of absence."

"His grandfather died," Alison said. "He left to help his grandmother."

Mr. Morgan raised his eyebrows. Before he could leave, Alison added, "Mr. Morgan, do I have enough money to buy the building my shop is in?"

Mr. Morgan laughed. At least Alison assumed it was laughter. At any rate, his chest rattled a little and his mouth twisted. "My dear girl, certainly."

"Good," she mumbled. He left with another muffled snicker. With a sigh of relief Alison leaned back against the closed door. The day seemed as though it had lasted a month, and it still wasn't over. Her head was pounding, and Jamie was up way past his bedtime.

The clock struck ten. Alison pushed herself away from the door and walked to the kitchen.

She heard him whistling even before she entered the room. He was at the sink, finishing up the last of the dishes, one of Mrs. Potter's old aprons tied under his arms, his jacket off, his shirtsleeves rolled up to his elbows, his hands immersed in suds.

"You make a very domestic picture," Alison said.

"Just trying to impress the boss," he quipped.

She tried to smile, but her head hurt too much. "Where's Jamie?"

"He took a shower by himself. I read him a story and tucked him in."

Alison leaned back against the counter. She was relieved Jamie was already in bed but disappointed she hadn't had a chance to talk to him first. "Thank you. You didn't have to do that tonight, and you certainly didn't have to do these dishes. I could have. Wait a minute. Grace comes in tomorrow. I suppose this is the kind of thing we should leave for her."

"You're new at this, aren't you?" he asked as he pulled the drain plug. He took off the apron and wiped his hands on the soft cloth.

"New at what?"

"At being wealthy."

Alison nodded slightly. "A babe in the woods," she admitted. "Did Jamie remember to feed Nora?"

"We did it together. She loves peanut butter, by the way."

Alison put her fingers on her temples and pushed. "She eats anything. Was dinner really as bad as I think it was?"

"Possibly worse. Headache?"

"Hmm—"

"Give me your hands."

"Why?"

"Come on," he coaxed. "Who can you trust if not your nanny? Give me your hands."

Slowly she put her hands into Jack's. His were amazingly warm and soft from the dishwater. "This is something I learned from one of my students. It's called acupressure. Does your head hurt on both sides?"

"Yes," she mumbled.

He moved his fingers slowly, steadily near the base of each thumb. "Left palm for right side of your head, right palm for left. I can't remember the exact spot, so I'll just massage the whole area between your wrist and your love line. Did you know you have a very long love line?"

"Another student taught you how to read palms?"

"Certainly. Close your eyes. Try to relax. I'll support your hands."

Alison closed her eyes, concentrating on the warm pressure of his fingers and trying to relax, but he was standing very close. She could even smell the spicy aroma of his after-shave, but it was the strength and rhythm of his fingers massaging her hands that held her. After a few seconds she felt light-headed.

"Now to bed," he said softly.

Her eyes flew open. Jack smiled. "Go on up to bed and get some sleep. Your headache will go away, but it may take a while."

"Thank you," she mumbled. "I do feel better."

"Good." He was unrolling his sleeves, buttoning his cuffs. She watched him and wondered what exactly she'd gotten herself into.

"When shall I report in for work, boss?" he asked.

"Whenever you can."

"Monday morning?"

"Fine. I have an appointment Monday afternoon. Do you suppose you can pick Jamie up from school at one-thirty? I just sold the Mercedes, but I can—"

"I have my own car, thanks. I'll be happy

to pick him up." He shrugged on his jacket and held the kitchen door open.

"This really is some house," he said.

Alison didn't respond to that. She knew her dislike of the house was irrational. "I've got to put the dog in the garage," she said.

"Already done," Jack told her. "Jamie is really something, know that? I mean, the kid is only six, and he remembered Nora. I like him, Alison."

She felt her heart swell with tenderness again. Maybe this would work, after all.

" 'Course, he needs a little toughening up," he mused. "Been pampered too much."

"We'll see."

"Monday," Jack promised; then he was gone.

Chapter Five

*A*lison balanced precariously atop the eight-foot ladder, one hand grasping a branch of curly willow, the other wielding pruning shears. She'd awakened to a drizzly Monday morning but couldn't stand the thought of spending it in the house. After she drove Jamie to school, she came back and hauled the ladder from the garden shed, Grace's shocked face regarding her from the kitchen window. At the housekeeper's insistence Alison agreed to tie Nora to the trunk of a small nearby tree. All she needed was a seventy-pound dog galloping under the ladder.

Sunday had passed lazily, Alison content to spend two hours in the den reading the paper while Jamie watched a movie on the VCR, and Grace did whatever it was Grace did. The most energetic thing Alison had done was brush Nora to a red-gold sheen. And despite her hovering around the phone like an adolescent girl waiting for a prom date, Mr. Singleton hadn't called.

Toward evening Jamie, Nora, and Alison walked to the shop where Chris had left the van. All three of them had hamburgers for dinner at a drive-through restaurant. They even stopped by the grocery store to buy a box of Space Chunks breakfast cereal and a new tube of toothpaste!

The pile of branches under the tree grew more impressive as Alison continued to trim. She had only one little section left to do.

"Someone should be holding this ladder."

She looked down, surprise making her wobbly. Jack caught her ankles, steadying her.

"I was fine till you startled me," she admonished.

"Sorry. Let me hold this for you." He moved his hands from her ankles to the ladder sides. "Do you always prune your own trees?"

"This is the first time I've had a tree to prune," she told him. It was a little unnerving to have him standing beneath her, and Alison spent a moment wishing she'd pulled on something more flattering than gray sweatpants and a windbreaker.

"What are you going to do with all these branches?" he asked.

She snipped the last branch and looked down. Tiny beads of moisture clung to his hair, misted his glasses. He was dressed in jeans and his leather jacket and looked more like one of his students than a professor.

"I'm going to load a few into my van and take them into the shop. The rest will have to wait till the gardener comes later this week. I guess he'll haul them away."

She handed the pruning shears down to Jack, who kept a hand on her leg as she descended the ladder. It was disconcerting, to say the least, to have him that close, to feel the warmth of his hand through the fabric. She'd given her feelings, her attraction for him, a lot of thought on Sunday and decided it was absolutely imperative that she maintain a professional manner around him. Now she admitted it might not be so easy.

Jack folded the ladder together and hefted it onto his shoulder. "Where to?"

"Let me take that thing," she told him. "It'll get your jacket dirty."

"Alison, please. I'm trying to impress you with my virility."

"By picking up a ladder?"

"There are no dragons to slay, so I'll move the ladder. Where to?"

"The shed behind the garage. I left the lock off."

He nodded and left. Alison picked deftly through the branches, quickly trimming the best ones. She put the stripped ends into a tall bucket half filled with water, working till the pail was crowded with twigs. They were going to look wonderful in arrangements, their dark, twisted branches such a contrast to the soft symmetry of the flowers.

"You're humming," Jack said.

"Do you always sneak up on people?"

He grinned. He'd let Nora off her leash. She cavorted on the grass, throwing broken branches into the air for herself. She was already dirty again. "Sorry. You just looked so content. I don't think I've seen you look that happy."

Alison shrugged. "I guess I was a million miles away," she admitted.

"Let me take that pail for you. Do you want it in your van?"

"That's right, but really, I can—"

He glared at her. "Please. I'm still slaying dragons."

"I didn't hire you to slay dragons," she reminded him as she fell into step beside him. "I hired you to take care of Jamie."

"As I will when he's here. This your van?

It's cute." He tilted his head to the side and added, "Who's the other heart?"

"I beg your pardon?"

" 'Two Hearts Florist,' " he read. "I assume you're one heart. Who's the lucky guy?"

"My mother named the shop. The two hearts were hers and Dad's." He smiled slowly, and rather than speculating on exactly what that smile meant, Alison changed the subject.

"I never figured you for a truck," she said, nodding toward the battered green Ford that sat beside her van. She opened the van's double back doors and pushed the plywood frame that accommodated vases out of the way. Nora's sensitive nose must have picked up the lingering scent of last night's hamburgers, because she made a frantic effort to jump in the van. Alison caught hold of her collar while Jack loaded the pail, then slammed the doors.

"What did you figure me for?" he asked.

For a long moment she stared at Jack, and he stared at her. She couldn't help wondering if he found her attractive. He seemed to joke around with everyone, comfortable with people as diverse as Jamie and Mr. Morgan. It was that easygoing charm that attracted her. He took off his glasses to wipe the lenses with a clean handkerchief, and Alison got her first good look at his eyes. They were dark and deep like Jamie's. He met her gaze till she felt absorbed and glanced away, breaking the spell.

"I don't know," she mumbled. "A sports car, I guess. Well, are you ready to move in?"

He set his glasses back on his nose. "Teachers don't make enough money to buy sports cars. At least, I don't. My stuff is in the house. Grace said to wait till you came in. I don't think she knows where to put me."

Alison nodded as she moved away, her first steps stiff, as though she'd been rooted to the ground for hours instead of seconds. Jack came along with her.

"Stay," she told Nora, who ignored her.

"The mutt is filthy," Jack said as he patted the dog's head. "How in the world do you wash her?"

"Mavis actually paid the dog-grooming shop to come here and shampoo her. I guess they bring the whole operation along. It proves what can be accomplished with enough money."

"Then why don't you call them?" he asked, closing the door on Nora's eager face.

"Because she's a dog," Alison explained. Apparently he didn't understand that she wasn't quite as frivolous with money as Mavis had been. "I can't spend over a hundred dollars to have a dog bathed, especially a dog that redirties almost instantly. As soon as it warms up, I'll scrub her down outside."

"You're incredible," he said softly, but by the time she'd recovered from the shock of hearing his words, he'd turned around, and she wasn't sure he'd meant it as a compliment.

"All I need is a bed, a desk, and decent lighting," Jack said as they climbed the stairs. She was carrying his suitcase. He was lugging a huge box of papers. Alison had managed to peek at the top one before he whisked the box away. It was covered with writing; unfortunately, the writing wasn't English.

"This room is Jamie's," she told him as they passed the first door. "I put you here." She opened the third door down the landing. The room was big and light, decorated mostly in black and white with touches of blue. The room that Mavis had always assigned to the nannies was closer to Jamie's, but it was hopelessly feminine, with enough pink and flounce to make most men shudder.

"It's . . . modern," Jack said as he looked around. Then he saw the desk. "Oh, this is really great." He dropped the box on top of the oak monster and touched the wood lovingly with his fingers.

Alison nodded toward the box. "Is that the 'project' you mentioned?"

He sat on the edge of the desk. He opened his mouth, closed it, opened it again and said, "Yes."

"Why are you so secretive?" she asked him idly. Actually, the question wasn't idle at all. She just wanted it to sound that way.

His glance was sharp. He cleared his throat. "I don't know what you're talking about. I'm not secretive."

"Yes, you are," she persisted. "I know it's none of my business, but you've made it like a puzzle, and now I can't help being curious. Throw me a bone. Are you working on a book? Is it your family tree or love letters from some famous movie star? Come on, give me a hint."

"No," he snapped. "Of course not. No."

"I think he doth protest too much," she said, adding, "Okay, so I misquote Shakespeare."

Jack cleared his throat again. "Alison, please, I don't want to talk about it."

"Yes, professor," she said primly, then laughed. He looked startled, but he joined her.

"Okay. It's really no big deal. I . . . found a . . . well, a stack of papers, really, a chronicle of Grandfather's life while he was a young man in Russia. I found it when I was helping Gram clean out Grandfather's den. He was born in the old country, and the diary is written in Russian. Gram can't read Russian, but he taught me how. Anyway, she wanted me to translate it for her."

He paused and looked at his hands. Alison was suddenly sorry she'd pried. She set his suitcase down, ready to leave once he looked up. Instead, he added, "There are certain . . . things I've found. I don't yet know the full meaning of these . . . things."

"But they bother you?" she prompted.

"Yes," he said, looking up. "They bother me."

"And you don't want to talk about it anymore."

"Not right now," he agreed. "Mind?"

"Not at all. By the way, there's a library in the den downstairs. You're welcome to use it anytime." She glanced at her watch. "Listen, I really have to take a quick shower and drive to the shop. I'll be gone most of the afternoon."

"We need to discuss what you expect of me," Jack said.

"Yes, I suppose we do. I don't have time now."

"Tonight?"

"Yes. Okay, tonight."

"Any errands you want run?" he asked.

"If it wouldn't be any trouble. Jamie needs shoes, any kind he wants. Mavis had charge accounts, which I seem to have inherited, in every store and restaurant in town, so go where you want. Mr. Morgan called me this morning to tell me that you checked out clean enough to run for Pope, and I asked him to put your name on the accounts. Oh, and maybe could you do something about dinner just this once? Send out for pizza or something? Grace lives at home, so it's just Jamie, you, and me."

"Do you mean our only chaperon is a six-year-old child?"

"Are you afraid I'll compromise your good name?" Alison teased.

"Well, no, of course not. I just thought you might feel uneasy. . . . This is coming out all wrong."

Alison leaned against the doorjamb. "Mr. Morgan had you checked out clear back to your birth. If I am going to trust you with Jamie, then I can certainly trust your integrity. I've got to go."

Jack nodded. "Grace can answer any of my questions, right?"

"I don't know," Alison admitted. "I suppose she can." With that admittedly ambiguous response, she rushed off down the hall.

A half hour later she inspected her reflection in the mirror. She'd pass, Alison decided, a little surprised at how nervous she felt at the prospect of meeting with Courtney Howell. As she adjusted her straight black skirt, she wondered again how Courtney had heard of Two Hearts Florist. No matter. After a social event like this wedding, who knew what business would start pouring in?

"You look nice," Grace said as Alison searched for her coat. The housekeeper opened the closet and took the coat off a hanger. Alison was still unused to someone putting her things away when she wasn't looking. "I like your sweater," Grace added. "The blue matches your eyes."

"Thanks," Alison told her. It was amazing how quickly Grace had warmed up once Mrs. Potter left. Alison wanted to add that Grace was free to wear something other than that horrible blouse and jumper to work, but she didn't want to hurt the woman's feelings. Maybe they were all she could afford. Alison made a mental note to tell Mr. Morgan to give her a raise. "You've met Jack?"

Grace actually blushed a little. "Yes."

Alison looked harder at her, and the housekeeper blushed deeper. "He's a flirt, isn't he?" she commented.

Grace's eyes blinked rapidly a couple of times, and she stuttered, "Yes, well . . . he's a kidder, all right."

"Well, just help him find things. He'll take

care of Jamie. Now, I've got to go. You decoy Nora at the kitchen door with a scrap or something while I dash to my van, okay?"

"On my way," Grace said.

A few seconds later Alison escaped out the front door.

Two Hearts Florist was located in a two-story building in downtown Eureka. Alison had bought the business from her father when he announced that now, with Mom gone and Alison all grown up, he'd decided to sell out and retire to Alaska where he'd heard the salmon jump into your boat all by themselves.

Alison parked the van in the alley and took the bucket of curly willow in through the back door. The building was long and narrow. The back of the bottom floor was taken up with a sink, walk-in refrigerator for the flowers, and work space for the designers, where Deanne was busy working on a project.

"Oooh," Deanne said when she saw the bucket. She grabbed it from Alison and started sorting through the branches.

Alison walked out front and nodded at Chris, who was busy ringing up a sale. The front housed the sales counter, a small display refrigerator, and racks and shelves of everything from mugs to fine china, silk flowers to one-of-a-kind lamps.

The shop was still overflowing with red hearts and other Valentine Day goodies, all marked down fifty percent. Soon they would stow what was left upstairs and bring down the Easter goods. The top floor was storage, and in the back, the apartment Alison had called home for four years till Mavis's tragedy had thrust her headlong into Jamie's life.

She took a tiny stuffed panda from the shelf and went back to the workroom.

"Boy, do you look swank!" Deanne said. "Good thing, too, 'cause the society princess and her mother have been calling here every hour on the hour wanting to talk to you."

"Never fear, the cavalry has arrived," Alison said as she hung her coat on a hook. Deanne was arranging yellow gladiolus and huge white pom-pom chrysanthemums. Alison admired her work, then peeked in the walk-in refrigerator where buckets were a third full of roses, irises, carnations, tulips, daffodils, and several other varieties of flowers. Good thing Sam came in the morning. The cold little room brightened her heart, the ferns, mosses, and flowers a heady, fragrant, constant delight.

They both heard the outside door open at the same time. Deanne made a face. Chris came into the workroom and announced Courtney Howell's arrival.

"This woman means big bucks, big publicity," Alison whispered to Deanne. "Treat her as though she's as good as she thinks she is."

"No one is as good as she thinks she is," Deanne whispered back, but she plastered a smile on her face and preceded Alison out front.

Chapter Six

*C*hris was busy helping a customer. When she met Alison's gaze, she nodded toward the corner where two women stood apart from everything.

The older woman saw Alison and stepped forward. She was a short woman with expertly dyed apricot hair that almost perfectly matched the color of her wool suit. Some poor little animal had given his all for the fur stole draped stylishly across one shoulder. She held out a gloved hand.

"Miss Simmons? I am Lillian Howell, and this is my daughter, Courtney. Please, accept our sympathy over the accident that claimed poor little Mavis."

Alison shook her hand and nodded. Mavis would have hated being referred to in those particular terms, but the sentiment was kind. She smiled at Courtney.

Courtney Howell was taller than her mother and thinner. Her hair was a natural version of her mother's, but twisted high on her head in a style too old for her twenty or so years. She regarded Alison with a steady green-eyed gaze and would have been pretty if her mouth wasn't set in what appeared to be a permanent pout. She didn't acknowledge Alison's smile.

"You're here for a much happier occasion," Alison said.

"Yes, yes," Mrs. Howell gushed. "Courtney is marrying."

"Have you set a date?"

"December," Courtney said. "I want a Christmas wedding. Barton is accepting a job in London that begins next February, so we're going to honeymoon in Europe." She spoke slowly, her gaze directed to a spot three inches under Alison's left ear.

"How thrilling!" Alison told her.

Courtney smiled. The smile didn't touch her icy-green eyes. Deanne handed Alison an order form for wedding flowers.

"Have you decided where the wedding and reception will be held and what colors you'll include?" Alison asked as she filled in Courtney's and Barton Fielding's names.

Courtney examined her fingernails. Mrs. Howell volunteered information. "The rehearsal dinner will be held at The Golden Unicorn. The wedding will be at St. Paul's. The reception will be held at Mr. Howell's club. Then, of course, we'll need flowers at our home and at the hotel where Barton's family will be staying." She snapped open her purse and extracted several swatches of cloth in varying colors. "The neutrals are my home, the blue and gold the restaurant, the yellow and green plaid Mr. Howell's club, and the red lace what Courtney insists her wedding party will wear. I suppose the men's boutonnieres will have to be red too."

Alison clipped the fabric to her form and made notes. Mrs. Howell continued, undaunted, "Courtney will have eight bridesmaids—"

"Six, Mother."

"No, dear, eight."

Fire momentarily blazed in Courtney's eyes, then was just as quickly dampened. "I will not have Tammy and Vanessa as bridesmaids."

"They are your cousins," Mrs. Howell snarled.

"Tammy is way too skinny, and Vanessa is a myopic little snitch."

Part of Alison wanted to laugh. Was this for real? Part of her wanted to crawl under the counter.

"You will have them, and that's all there is to it," Mrs. Howell said firmly. Quite firmly.

"Well," Alison said, "it's going to be quite an affair, isn't it? Good thing we have several months to plan."

"The social event of the season," Mrs. Howell agreed. "Courtney's colors will be red and white."

"I like wildflowers," Courtney said.

"That's ridiculous," Mrs. Howell sniffed.

"Actually, wildflowers can be charming," Alison said, though why she was standing up for Courtney Howell was beyond her. Before Mrs. Howell could thunder, Alison added, "Unfortunately, there aren't many around here in December."

Courtney looked in Alison's eyes. It occurred to Alison that she might not be quite as self-assured as she pretended to be. "Tulips, then," Courtney said.

Tulips in December. "I can probably get them through South America," Alison mused aloud.

"And I want flowers on the cake," she added.

"Now, Courtney. I thought we decided not to put fresh flowers on the cake."

"You decided," Courtney amended. "I want flowers."

"It's too informal for a wedding like yours, dear," Mrs. Howell said.

"That's just it, isn't it, Mother? It's my wedding and Barton's. I want flowers on the cake."

"As I said," Alison reminded them softly, "there's lots of time to iron out the details. Shall we fill out this form?"

For the next hour they filled in the spaces or tried to. Mother and daughter disagreed on almost everything. Deanne got sick of their bickering and went to the back to work on flower arrangements. Alison just filled in the blanks, crossed them out, and filled them in again.

They were almost finished when Courtney threw the last wrench into the works. "I want everything to be unique," she said with more passion then she'd shown so far. "I want huge red baskets of flowers everywhere, and I want my bouquet to be like this." Here she circled her arms like a basketball hoop. "Huge."

Mrs. Howell shook her head. "That's garish."

"Baskets can be lovely," Alison placated. "Next time you come in, I'll have some pictures for you to look at. It'll help you decide."

"I already have," Courtney proclaimed with a defiant look at her mother. "I read that brides in China wear red. I like that."

Mrs. Howell sighed heavily.

"Fine." Alison slipped their form back under the clip, anxious to have this little session with the Howells come to an end. Of course, as time passed, there would have to be more sessions, but since they had several months to do it in, Alison gave herself a break. "Thanks for coming in," she added.

Mrs. Howell patted her hair. "Well, I knew Mavis, of course. Socially, you know."

"You inherited all her money, didn't you?" Courtney asked.

Mrs. Howell gasped in shock at her daughter's breach of etiquette.

Alison smiled and said, "Some of it. Most of her estate went to her son, of course."

"Then why do you work . . . here?"

"Courtney Howell!"

"It's all right," Alison told told them both, but she could feel two little hot spots forming high over her cheekbones. "This is my shop. I love working here. I don't believe I'd ever be very good at being one of the idle rich."

Mrs. Howell was now almost as uncomfortable as Alison was. Courtney met Alison's gaze with her cool green one, but Alison sensed the beginnings of a thaw.

"Oh."

"It's why we came here," Mrs. Howell

added, intending to placate Alison. "I just knew your being related to Mavis Dufour would mean you'd have good taste."

"Thank you," Alison said, but her heart sank a little. She'd hoped all her hard work and expensive advertising had compelled the Howells to give Two Hearts a chance. She should have known it would somehow tie into Mavis and her money.

"One more thing," Mrs. Howell said softly, but there was steel in her voice. "Every aspect of this wedding must be perfect, and that includes the flowers. I will not have the Fieldings laughing behind our backs at this little hick town Tom insists we live in."

"Daddy likes all the redwood trees," Courtney explained.

"Yes, well, I suppose that's part of it. Do you understand, Miss Simmons?"

"Perfectly," Alison told her and didn't breathe easily again until the door had closed behind them.

"Whew!" she said under her breath.

Deanne had come up behind Alison. "Quite a pair, aren't they?"

"Yes. They're probably fine alone, but together—"

"They're snobs, Alison, plain and simple. And snobs or not, you handled them just right.

I would have thrown the two of them out on their well-clad tails."

"No, you wouldn't have."

"Oh, yes," she insisted. "I mean it, Alison. You've acquired some class since living in that mansion. You handled the whole thing perfectly." She grinned and added, "Can't you just picture little Miss Society tripping down St. Paul's aisle on her father's arm clad in a red wedding gown?"

Alison smiled but felt vaguely troubled. Oh, not about the color of the gown—she knew Mrs. Howell would nip that idea in the bud. Had she really changed, though? Was that good?

Deanne cut speculation short by pushing a stack of phone messages in front of her. "Okay, boss lady, back to work."

"Did Mr. Singleton call?"

"Not here. Didn't he get to you over the weekend?"

"No."

"He will," she assured Alison.

Alison didn't think she was really worth much that afternoon. For one thing, she was worried about the Howell wedding. How "different" did this girl want to be, and could she think of something avant garde enough to satisfy her and not alienate her mother and the rest of the community? Alison preferred traditional flowers at weddings. The real reason people gathered was to wish Godspeed to the newlyweds who were pledging their hearts and souls to each other. Nothing should upstage the joyous solemnity of such an occasion. Flowers and music were to enhance the ceremony, not overwhelm it.

She also kept thinking about Mr. Singleton. Why hadn't he called? Surely he knew she was now in the position to make him an offer on his building.

Most important, however, she kept thinking about Jack and Jamie. How were they getting along? Would she go home to leather shoes and tears? Alison's heart had always been in this shop, and it had always been enough. Now, suddenly, it wasn't, and she felt divided in a totally mysterious way.

It was dark by the time Alison got home. She'd been ready to leave earlier, but at the last moment a quiet, middle-aged woman had come into the shop to apply for the job as flower designer. Deanne and Alison worked with Shirley Hobbs for an hour or so. She was meticulous, creative, self-effacing, and, best of all, didn't mind working overtime. Now Alison wouldn't feel so guilty asking Deanne to cover for her.

The house smelled so good that for a moment Alison was afraid Mrs. Potter was back. She flung her coat over a chair and walked back to the kitchen.

Jack and Jamie were seated at the kitchen table. Nora was under the table, sitting like a yellow sphinx. An orange, a Ping-Pong ball, and what appeared to be a frozen pea were suspended by an intricate design of string from the low ceiling-light fixture over the table. Two dark heads swiveled, and one yellow tail swept the tile as Alison pushed open the door.

Jamie smiled briefly. Jack's smile was brighter and longer lasting.

"You're home. Good. Dinner is almost ready."

"Looks delicious," Alison said, pointing at the weird assortment dangling above the table.

Jamie giggled. Jack shook his head. "Dinner, m'lady, consists of prime rib, baked potatoes, and string beans. These goodies represent the sun, the earth, and the moon."

"The solar system," Jamie announced proudly. He got up on his knees and perched on the edge of the table. He blew on the Ping-Pong ball, which was rigged to circle the orange while the pea rotated around it.

"Very impressive," Alison said.

Jack stood, lifted Jamie to the floor, and told him to go wash for dinner.

"Wait a second," Alison interrupted. "Jamie Dufour, let me have a look at you. Are those Nikes on your two feet?"

Jamie giggled again. Two giggles in one day!

"And are you wearing jeans and a genuine T-shirt with a picture of a motorcycle on it? Wow!"

"That's okay, isn't it?" Jack asked. "I mean, I thought the kid and I could toss a ball around after school. He didn't have any jeans."

"I don't think he even has a ball. Do you, Jamie?"

Jamie shook his head. He looked exactly six years old. Alison ruffled his hair before he could jerk away and said, "Better get him a ball tomorrow."

"Right," Jack said.

She brought her left hand from behind her back and gave Jamie the little panda she'd chosen earlier that afternoon. She'd put him in a mug with bright-red carnations and white bows.

Jamie took the panda, a shy smile drawing up the corners of his mouth.

"I forgot to bring you a Valentine Day present last Friday," Alison explained. "When the flowers get old, you can use the mug for hot chocolate or milk."

"Thank you, Cousin Alison," he said softly. For one brief moment his eyes met hers; then he ran off to his room. Nora scrambled to her feet and followed.

Alison sank down onto Jamie's vacated chair. "It smells wonderful in here," she said wearily. "You brushed Nora, didn't you? Thanks. Give me a second, and I'll go set the table."

"Would you mind just eating here?" Jack asked.

"Not at all. To tell you the truth, this room always kind of intimidated me, but now that Mrs. Potter is gone, I've begun to grow quite fond of it. And, Jack, thanks for cooking dinner. I promise I'll find us a cook."

Jack sat down opposite her. "Alison, I was thinking. I know a house like this takes a lot of upkeep and that Jamie is used to having servants around. I know you don't know how to cook. But I do. Let me keep the refrigerator stocked. We'll have simple meals, nothing fancy. What do you think?"

She was glad he realized she wasn't used to this life-style. "Do you have any idea how many more hours a day it will take you to shop and cook? What about your project?"

"Let me worry about my project," he said seriously. "Cooking can't take all that much time. Tonight's dinner was a cinch."

Alison decided not to point out that Mrs. Potter had shopped for this dinner. "If you really want to do it, I'd love it. And Jamie will have to make a few minor adjustments as time goes by. The truth of the matter is that his life will never be exactly the same again. I'll keep this house for him till he's recovered from the shock of losing his mother, but I'm not going to spend my life in this place. It's too big, and I have the shop to care for too. He and I don't need six bedrooms and servants' quarters."

"But it's really a great house," Jack protested.

Alison took a deep breath. "I know it is. Mavis was very proud of it. I hope I can hold on to it till Jamie is old enough to make a decision about it for himself."

Jack studied his hands for a second; then very softly he said, "I've never told you, Alison, and I should have. I'm sorry about your cousin. It must have been awful to lose someone so young."

"Yes," Alison agreed slowly. "It was. Maybe not so much for what was as what will never have a chance to be. I don't suppose that makes any sense."

"It does," he assured her. "And I know it's none of my business, but can't you afford to keep this house as long as you want?"

Alison supposed she should have been offended by his question—but she owed him one after nosing into his business that afternoon. Besides, his voice held curiosity touched with concern, so she didn't mind. "Money," she began. "When you don't have it, it's everything. Mavis had it, and she was never happy. I'm just beginning to realize that the most important thing she had wasn't a thing at all, but a person, and she all but abandoned him. Nope, money isn't the key to happiness. You can't just wad up dollar bills and throw them at problems and make them go away."

"So what do you want?" Jack asked.

Alison thought for a second. "I want to make Jamie happy. I want to live simply and somehow give him a meaning to his life so he isn't empty inside when he grows up." Unbidden, she thought of Courtney Howell and shuddered. "I want him to love me. And I want to somehow merge my family—Jamie—with my work, which is what makes me happy inside. Is that too much to ask?"

"Always 'Jamie and me,'" Jack said as he rose to open the oven. "Don't you ever plan on getting married and having another child?

Jamie would love a sister or a brother, to say nothing of a father."

"And how do you know that?" Alison asked as she kicked off her shoes. She was pleased he'd said "another."

"He told me." He took the roast out of the oven and added, "You didn't answer my question."

"Yes," she said, smiling at the picture of him holding the pan in two mitt-covered hands, Mrs. Potter's apron tied under his arms. "I want to marry and have children. But first I have to find the right guy."

"Always a hitch, huh?" he quipped.

"If it's not one thing, it's another," she agreed. "Boy, am I starving!"

"Go get Jamie while I put dinner on the table," he directed over his shoulder.

Alison grinned at his back and went to find Jamie.

After a dinner even Mrs. Potter would have been proud of, Alison insisted on stacking the dishes for Grace. She still wasn't sure how much she should leave for the housekeeper to do, but she couldn't stand the thought of dirty dishes all over the table.

It was well after eight by the time she went upstairs. She looked in Jamie's room. Jamie was curled up in his bed, his ears and cheeks pink from the tub. Jack sat on a chair beside the bed, reading. He'd taken his glasses off and looked up when Alison stopped by the open door. The sight of the two of them caused an unexplained lump to form in Alison's throat.

"Alison, come sit over here by Jamie."

"I don't want to intrude," she said softly.

"We're getting to the good part," Jack insisted. "Aren't we, Jamie?"

Alison watched Jamie closely. He looked at her, his face an unreadable little-boy mask, and shrugged. It was a shrug of dismissal.

"Thanks, anyway," she told them breezily. " 'Night, honey. See you in the morning." She blew Jamie a kiss and went back downstairs before Jack could see the tears well up in her eyes.

She went back to the kitchen to make a pot of coffee, telling herself that it was okay, that she understood Jamie's reluctance to accept her. Nora's tail thumped against the glass door. Alison forgot the coffee and opened the door. The dog rushed into the kitchen, a large golden blur of fresh air and mud. Her feet skidded on the tile floor as she whirled around to press herself against Alison's legs.

Alison sank down to the floor, her arms full of dog. She buried her head against the damp fur, and tears she hadn't even realized were there filled her eyes and spilled down her cheeks. A quiet sob caught in her throat and then another. Nora whimpered. Alison patted the broad forehead and took a shaky deep breath while Nora licked a salty tear from Alison's chin.

"You're an old softy," she told the dog, who whimpered again. She wiped the rest of the tears from her face with her fingertips and sniffed. Maybe crying didn't solve anything, but it helped ease the hurt.

She had just gotten up off the floor when Jack came into the kitchen.

"Ah, I see Hurricane Nora is in," he said without looking directly at Alison. He began shoveling dry dog food into Nora's dish. Alison told him she'd meet him in the den when he was ready to discuss his duties, and she escaped.

Well, what did I want? she quizzed herself as she washed her face in the downstairs bathroom. *For the child to instantly call me Mom and accept me? He's been shuffled here and there most of his life, with a different nanny every few months, and now we tell him his mother isn't coming back, and bingo! he lives with me. How can I expect him to trust me immediately? How can I ask him to understand things that stump adults? I have to give him time, that's all. Time.* She looked into the mirror over the sink. Her face looked splotchy and red, her eyes bloodshot. Maybe Jack would think she drank.

By the time she got to the den, Jack was already sitting in a spindly little antique gold-colored chair beside the desk. Alison took several moments to close the drapes, restack books, and shuffle papers. By the time she sat down in the swivel chair, she was in control again.

"So, what do I do around here?" Jack asked.

"Care for Jamie," she said succinctly. "I'll cover Saturday mornings and Sundays. If you're positive you want to cook, then I guess you get to go to the store as well. Oh, Jamie has a counselor appointment twice a month late in the afternoon, so you'll need to take him to that too."

"What does he go to a counselor for? Specifically, I mean. Has he had nightmares?"

"No, nothing like that." Alison steeled herself for the same kind of criticism Mr. Morgan had voiced when she first insisted on counseling. "After Mavis died, I decided he should have someone to talk to, someone trained and impartial. He didn't see much of his mother, you know. She traveled extensively, and when she was home, one of the nannies or Mrs. Potter cared for him. Still, she was his mother, and I just thought—"

Jack held up his hand. "Good idea," he interrupted.

With a sigh Alison added, "I don't know if it's really helping."

"It can't hurt. What has the counselor said?"

"Oh, just that Jamie isn't as upset as most six-year-olds would be, because of the nature of his care. He might not even really understand Mavis won't come sweeping back into his life at some later date. She thinks he misses his nanny more."

"The one Mrs. Potter fired?"

"Yes," Alison said, still seething with anger over that woman's callousness. "Gretchen had been with Jamie for almost a year—that's a long time in this house. She and Mrs. Potter didn't get along. As soon as Mavis died, Mrs. Potter fired her. I tried to find her, to hire her back, but she'd taken another post immediately and was overseas by that time." Alison paused and studied her hands.

"What is it, Alison? What's wrong?"

She looked up at him and said, "I just hope I'm doing the right thing."

Jack leaned closer and put his hand over hers. The shift of his weight prompted groans of protest from the fragile chair. "I think you're doing great."

"He . . . he seems so close to you in such a short period of time," she said, wincing at the jealousy she could hear in her voice.

Jack shrugged. "I'm a stranger, a big man with funny glasses."

"No," she said, meeting his eyes. "It's more than that. You have a way with people. I've felt it myself."

He smiled. "Trust yourself. Give Jamie time. He's going to be wild about you—trust me. No man can resist a woman who brings him flowers." He hesitated a moment and added, "Did you see what was wrapped up in his arms under the covers?"

Alison looked down at her hands. "No."

Jack mumbled something softly to himself, then stood abruptly. He walked over to the shelves of books and turned his back to them. Both his hands were shoved deep into his pockets, and his face was half hidden by shadows. When he spoke, his voice was soft. "He had your little panda all scrunched up under his chin."

Alison felt the tears threatening to roll again. She nodded gently, grateful beyond words that he'd told her.

"So you see," Jack continued, stepping closer, "everything is going to work out."

"Maybe Mr. Morgan is right," Alison said. "Maybe I should sell the shop."

Jack sat back down in the chair. "Now, why in the world would you do that?"

"Because then I could stay home with Jamie all the time."

"It's your decision," Jack said, "but if you ask me, you'd be making a big mistake. You'd be turning your back on yourself. That won't do Jamie any good. You can afford good help, not like a lot of people who have to worry about things like that. And now that Mrs. Potter's gone, I bet they won't all quit on you."

She half smiled. "You never even met the poor woman."

"But the stories I've heard!"

"How about you?" Alison half whispered. "Are you going to quit on me?"

"I've just begun," Jack said. There was something in his voice, some hint of meanings only guessed at. Alison decided to let the issue drop.

The phone rang. Jack stood amidst creaks and groans. "I'm going to go work for a while," he said. "Good night, Alison."

She watched him leave, then picked up the phone. Mr. Singleton's husky voice filled her ear. He told her exactly what he'd told Deanne, then paused. That was when Alison stuck in her two bits.

"I want to buy the building," she said quickly. "I'll pay whatever you're asking."

Mr. Singleton cleared his throat. "I'm sorry, Miss Simmons, I really am. Your father and I were fishing buddies for a long time, and I hate to disappoint you, but I've already sold."

"How could you?" she wailed.

"Now, don't fret. There are other buildings."

"But I'm established in yours," she explained.

"Yes, that's true, but like I said, I sold it. Truth of the matter is, I sold it to my wife's brother. He wants to open a restaurant. Perfect location, he says, and the wife agrees, and before you know it, there we are. 'Course, your lease is good for another six months."

"Of course," Alison said wearily.

"Real glad you understand," Mr. Singleton sputtered and hung up before she could say another word.

Six months? She was supposed to be relocated in six short months?

"Alison?"

She looked up to see Jack standing in the doorway. "Are you all right?" he asked.

"Yes," she lied. "I thought you were going to work on your book."

"I am. Thought I might borrow your cousin's library for a while if it isn't an inconvenience. I noticed she had a book on the Russian Revolution."

Alison waved toward the crowded shelves. "Be my guest. I was just on my way up to bed."

She passed very close to him. For a few seconds they stared at each other; then he put out his arm and folded her in a comfortable hug. "Sleep tight," he whispered against her hair.

She thought maybe he kissed the top of her head, but she wasn't sure. All she was sure of was that his arms were warm and strong, and she had to force herself to leave.

"Good night," she muttered, hoping Jamie didn't mind sharing his nanny.

Chapter Seven

*A*lison loved the spring. For one thing it was a great time for business, what with the busiest holiday of the year, Mother's Day, right on the heels of Easter. For another, each morning brought a new sign of change to nature—first crocuses, daffodils, tulips, and irises, followed by cherry and new growth on the giant redwoods.

Much to her chagrin, this year found her too busy to enjoy things the way she usually did. She spent half her time out of the shop, scouting new buildings. It was hard to believe Mr. Singleton was really selling out to his brother-in-law. For thirty years Two Hearts Florist had resided in the same downtown building. Alison's head swam when she thought of the ordeal of moving, to say nothing of the monumental task of informing the public where the shop had disappeared to.

Lucy Van Ness, the real estate broker Mr. Morgan recommended, finally found Alison a building a few blocks away from the present address. It wasn't as large or as airy, but the location wasn't bad, and it didn't look as though she had many choices. Alison delayed signing the papers, however, because she kept hoping something better would come along.

"Don't wait too long," Lucy Van Ness warned with a flash of her eyes. "You've got only a week to make up your mind. Remember, you can remodel to your heart's content because you'll own the building. I really believe this is an excellent property for your shop."

Alison told all of this to Deanne as she arranged two purple orchids in a shallow black enamel bowl. Across from her, the new designer, Shirley Hobbs, worked with white minicarnations and tiny yellow rosebuds, creating a delicate corsage for a frail elderly customer to wear on her ninetieth birthday. Both women listened to Alison, her business concerns, their concerns. All three heard the bell on the door ring, but since Chris was out front, they ignored it.

Seconds later a young woman looked in.

Courtney Howell nodded curtly. She was dressed in faded blue jeans, and her hair fell loose around her shoulders. She looked younger and prettier than she had the first time Alison met her.

"Hello," Alison said, straightening up.

"Hello," Courtney replied. She looked from Shirley to Deanne. Both of them smiled politely. Alison got the feeling Courtney was waiting for them to scurry away like obedient servants when the master of the house demands a conference.

"How may I help you?" Alison asked at last.

Courtney hitched her nose another rung higher in the air and said, "I want to discuss the flowers for my wedding."

Alison consulted the order form. "My supplier can get tulips in December from his distributor in Holland," she assured her. "As for the baskets and such, there won't be any problem. You and your mother can either buy them somewhere else and bring them in, or I'll order whatever you want. I've been researching unique weddings and have come up with a couple of ideas that might appeal to you. If you'll wait here a second, I'll dash upstairs and get the books to show you—"

"That's just it," Courtney interrupted. "I mean, I don't want baskets anymore, and I don't want tulips."

"Fine," Alison said evenly. If there was one

thing to be expected, it was this: brides change their minds. "Do you have any ideas—"

"I want lilacs. Tiffany, my maid of honor, says she saw lilacs at a wedding, and they were wonderful." She paused for a second and added, "Can you get lilacs in December?"

"I can try," Alison said doubtfully.

"Good. Mother said you'd laugh at me."

"It's your wedding," Alison reminded her. "All I want is for you to have everything the way you want it."

Courtney then said something that shocked Alison to the roots of her hair.

"Thank you."

When Alison recovered, she said, "You're welcome."

Courtney handed over a delicate swatch of lavender silk. "This is the new color of the wedding party. And here's a scrap of ribbon and lace from my gown. I'd like everything to match."

Alison took them from her and paper-clipped them to the order form. Out with the red lace, in with lilac and white. "I'll do my best," she assured Courtney, liking her a lot better when her mother wasn't around.

The back door opened, and Jamie's glossy head appeared. He grinned at the room in general. Jack came in behind him. Both of them were windblown and fresh as the flower buds that were popping out on fruit trees all over town.

"We were in your neck of the woods," Jack said.

"I got a new bike," Jamie chimed in. "It's silver."

"Hope we're not interrupting anything," Jack said.

"Not at all," Alison assured him. She'd already looked at the other faces in the room. Deanne's held playful assessment; Shirley's held mild curiosity and a certain amount of tenderness directed toward Jamie. Courtney was looking at Jack with awe. The other expressions Alison understood, but Courtney's baffled her, even though it reminded her of someone.

Alison introduced Shirley and Deanne. Shirley nodded shyly, but Deanne held out her hand. "So you're Jack? Strong grip—I like that in a man. My Ben's grip is like that. Say, the four of us ought to get together and have dinner sometime."

Alison groaned inwardly. Leave it to Deanne to treat her and Jack like a couple when they weren't. Jack seemed oblivious of her discomfort, however. "Sure," he said casually. "That would be great."

"Good!" Deanne said, smirking. At least to Alison it looked as though she were smirking. She handed Jamie a daisy.

"This is Courtney Howell," Alison said.

"Hello, Courtney," Jack said. "Are you reading any more Chekhov?"

Courtney smiled. This smile traveled into her eyes. "Hello, Professor Foxx. A little. I'm dropping out of school."

"I hate to hear that." Jack shook his head. "You're a good student."

"Courtney is getting married this winter," Alison told Jack. The awe was that of a student for a teacher, she decided, and the look that reflected that awe reminded her of the way Jamie looked at Jack.

He laughed. "You and Rob tying the knot, are you? That's great. Congratulations." He leaned forward and kissed her cheek briefly. "I always thought you two were a great couple."

Courtney turned scarlet. "She's marrying Barton Fielding," Alison said softly.

"Open mouth, insert foot," Jack said. He didn't look at all embarrassed, though. "Well, the congratulations still stand. You've known this guy a long time?"

She shrugged. "A few months."

He nodded, but his eyes looked worried, and

Alison filed that away. The man was a natural big brother to everyone.

Alison knelt down beside Jamie. "Did you say something about a new bike? May I see?"

He darted outside, and she followed, aware that everyone else was following too.

They all oohed and ahed over the bike, Jamie taking care to point out all the special features, like the horn and the shiny black tassels that hung from the handlebars.

"Hope it's okay, Alison," Jack whispered close to her ear. "His Scout group is getting ready for a bike jamboree at school. Jamie was the only kid without a bike. For that matter, he can't ride one, either. We're out practicing."

"Of course it's all right," she said, wishing she'd thought of it herself. "It's a great idea."

Jack smiled. His hand was warm on her arm. The sun was shining through a break in the stormy clouds overhead. It fell on Jack's hair like white paint. Alison swallowed hard, surprised at the depth of feelings that swirled and churned inside her, feelings that were becoming all too familiar but nonetheless confusing.

"Cousin Alison?"

Jamie's voice interrupted the tumultuous confusion Alison's thoughts had become. "Yes, sweetie?"

"Jack says we can have frozen pizza for dinner if it's okay with you."

"Sure. I'll be home early."

Jack helped Jamie mount his bike, keeping one hand on the handlebars and the other on the back of the banana seat. "Let's go, sport. We still have shopping to do. So long, ladies."

Deanne waved merrily, Courtney nodded, and Shirley shook her head as she retreated inside to work magic with her hands.

It was a week before Deanne mentioned Jack to Alison. She waited till they were alone after work; then she said, "Poor Jack. He doesn't stand a chance with you."

"And why is that?" Alison asked her.

"Because he doesn't resemble a daffodil, no way, no sir."

"And what makes you think he wants to have a chance with me?" Alison asked. "His only interest in me concerns Jamie."

Deanne laughed. "Right."

"I mean it, Deanne."

Deanne touched Alison's hand briefly. "You crazy flower lady. You really don't know, do you?"

"Know what?" Alison asked, a little bewildered.

"The way he looks at you when you're not

looking. The way you look at him when he's not looking."

"You have some imagination," Alison said. Her pulse was racing a little, though, because she knew that at least half of what Deanne said was true.

Deanne laughed again. "You're falling for him, aren't you?"

"You're crazy," Alison scoffed. She shrugged, the way Jamie did, the way that said she couldn't care less about something. "Besides, what would a college professor see in me? The man reads Russian, for heaven's sake."

"Oh, I don't know," Deanne drawled. She held up her hand and began ticking things off on her fingers. "Let's see. Number one, you're gorgeous. Number two, you're filthy rich even if you don't act it. Number three, you're smart. And number four, you're the kindest woman I know. What could he possibly see in you?"

"You're a real dreamer," Alison said slowly. "You're also the best friend a person could have."

"Right. I also want something."

"I should have guessed. What is it this time, a raise?"

"You gave us one of those last month. I want

you and Professor Hunk to come to dinner this weekend."

"Deanne—"

"It's just a dinner, Ali, and it's important to me."

"But Jamie—"

"Get Jack's grandmother to watch him for an evening, or that housekeeper—what's her name?"

"Grace."

"Right. Get her to stay over a night. Just come. Ben wants to see you, and we have a new recipe for shrimp-and-mushroom fettucini. Like I said, it's important to me."

Alison sighed. "I can't ask Jack to go out like that. It would be like a date or something, and it would be awkward. Besides, what's so important?"

Deanne examined her fingertips. "Come and find out. Anyway, I already asked Jack. He said he'd love to."

"You're awful."

Deanne nodded. "I know. So you're coming Saturday night?"

"Do I have a choice?" Alison asked. Deanne shook her head. "Then I guess I'm coming."

Alison walked home that night even though the sky was black with rain clouds and the wind blew cold along the sidewalk. For one thing, she needed time to think—did Jack really look at her when she wasn't looking? And for another, she was afraid to face Jack. What if he felt as though she had coerced him into this "date" by getting Deanne to ask them both to dinner? Why did the whole thing feel so seventh grade?

By the time Alison opened the gate, it was raining slanted drops and she had decided to cancel the dinner. Important to Deanne for some obscure reason or not, it was just too soon.

Jack's beat-up old truck was parked in the drive. Alison was disappointed Nora wasn't there to greet her, but the wily mutt must have convinced Jack and Jamie she was freezing to death and had to have refuge in the house. She was pretty good at looking pathetic through the glass door.

Alison eased the kitchen door open, expecting a big black wet nose to poke through at any second. None did. The kitchen was well lit and warm but empty. Alison slipped off her damp shoes and coat, then walked through the house, looking for Jack or Jamie . . . even Nora.

No one. She went back to the kitchen. The refrigerator was full, so Jack had been shopping. It looked as if they were having cold cuts for dinner. She took a bright red apple, polished it on her skirt, and leaned back against the counter. For years she'd come home to an empty apartment, and it hadn't bothered her a bit, but here she was alone for ten minutes, and she missed Jack's eyes, Jamie's giggle, Nora's thumping tail.

A hoot of laughter, followed closely by more hoots and a woof came from the basement stairwell. Alison opened the door and called, "Jack?"

"That you, Ali? Come on down. No, Brian, I told you to slow down. Jamie, put that over there, will you, sport?"

She put the apple on the counter, slipped on her damp shoes, and went downstairs.

They were narrow, steep stairs, but well lit. A heavy railing acted as a banister. The basement itself was one large room supported by eight large wooden pillars, skirted on the sides by smaller enclosures bathed in deep shadows. No one had ever done much with the basement. At one time wine and food had been stored at the base of the stairs, but Mavis had moved it all upstairs. Grace had confided to Alison that Mavis found the place "spooky."

Actually, though the corners were murky, the center of the room was well lit by a string of lights that straddled the pillars. High windows that needed a good washing were dark gray holes at the approaching night. They were set two-thirds of the way up the walls and looked out at the ground level of the yard.

If the basement had served any purpose over the last several years, it had been as a depository for broken furniture, old trunks, dusty toys, and nondescript cardboard boxes all taped shut. Most of this was pushed into the center of the room in a heap, though smaller piles were staggered all along the cement floor which had been swept halfheartedly.

Jack looked up when he heard Alison's footsteps. "Alison. Great. We need a crossing guard. Put this yellow apron on, hold this old Ping-Pong paddle, and stand. . . . Well, stand over there somewhere."

There were five little boys and one large man in the basement. There was also a large golden dog, complete with an old shoe in her mouth. The boys were dressed like all six-year-olds are dressed, even Jamie, thanks to Jack Foxx, in jeans. Their heads were covered with blue caps with gold braid and red-embroidered letters that read "Scout." Jack had on an identical cap, turned bill backward. He grinned and repeated, "Alison?"

All five boys had bikes. They were all red and blue and a little beat-up, except for Jamie's, which was gleaming silver.

Jack came over to Alison. "Surprised? Well, it's for the bike jamboree. Remember I told you about it? We need practice, and I thought with this big, empty room standing here, you wouldn't mind if we got in out of the weather." He dropped his voice and leaned closer. "By the way, don't let Jamie ride too close to you. He's still a little wobbly."

"Hi, Alison," Jamie said, grinning. He was straddling his bike like the other kids. She waved at him. It was the first time he had addressed her without using the word "cousin."

"Okay, group. Remember, Miss Simmons is the crossing guard. Oh, Alison, meet the guys. We're meeting here every Thursday, and we guarantee we'll meet outside unless it's raining like today. Let's see. That's John, Brian, Jamie—you know him—Brad and Tommy."

"Tony," a little red-haired imp corrected. "I'm Tony."

"Right, Tony. Sorry." He waved his arm and added, "Let's go."

Alison quickly stood where directed and held up the Ping-Pong paddle, green side for go, battered orange side for stop. The boys careened around the basement, around stacks of chairs, big trunks, empty barrels, and the pillars, stopping faithfully whenever she held up the orange side of the paddle. Alison concentrated on watching Jamie, who was wobbly, all right, but riding a bike.

An hour later Jack went upstairs and returned with an armload of apples.

"Take one home and eat it after dinner," he told the boys.

"We're supposed to snack right after school," Tony complained.

"We will," Jack promised, "but today we kind of forgot, and I don't want all your parents upset because you guys are too full to eat dinner."

The boys stuffed their apples into their pockets. Jack opened the outside door, then carried each bike up the stairs. It had stopped raining, but the magnolia tree released huge drops of collected water on their heads.

"They can't ride bikes home in the dark," Alison pointed out.

"You're right. Brian, you live next door, right? Ali, will you walk Brian home? I'll bring my truck around. The rest of you put your bikes in the back, and I'll give you a lift home. We're running a little late, so let's go!"

Jamie, Nora, and Alison walked Brian safely home. Jack wasn't back when they returned, so Alison took Jamie upstairs and ran a warm bath for him. She'd heard his teeth chattering. He babbled on endlessly about the afternoon, his defenses down so much that he even allowed Alison to hug him as she helped him towel dry.

After a dinner of cold sliced ham, fruit, and the inevitable fresh bread, Alison went down to the basement to make sure the door leading to the outside was locked. How could Mavis have thought the room spooky? It was heavily shadowed, but if the windows were cleaned and the place was properly lit, it would be charming. Alison thought it was a lot larger and a lot nicer than the places the real estate agent had shown her, easily twice as big as the building she'd signed the papers for earlier that week.

She wandered over to an old trunk and examined the hasp. It wasn't locked, so she opened the lid. The contents were difficult to see in the poor light but seemed to consist mostly of old clothes that smelled of mildew and mothballs. Curious, she dashed back upstairs and dug around in the kitchen till she found the flashlight. Jamie came into the kitchen as she was getting ready to go back downstairs, the mug she'd given him for Valentine Day clutched tightly in one hand.

"Going to bed?" she asked him.

He nodded. He pushed a chair over to the sink and poured himself a glass of water. Alison watched him. His pajamas were covered with red mice. With a jolt she realized she didn't feel tense or uncertain. Those emotions usually lurked in her stomach, coiled like a snake, waiting to spring the minute she and Jamie were alone. But tonight she felt only warmth and affection. Without pausing to think further, she put the flashlight down on the table and walked over to the sink.

"Good night, sweetie," she said softly.

Jamie looked up at her, then looked down at his fuzzy blue slippers and back up. "Jack says you got me my bike," he said.

Alison took a deep breath. "Actually, Jamie, Jack and I got you your bike, and your mom too."

"My mom is dead," he said firmly.

"Yes," she agreed, deciding that fact was a piece of reality that needed to be faced squarely. On the other hand, it was only half true. "Your mother is with you here," she said softly, touching Jamie's chest over his heart, "and in here." She tapped his head and added, "In your memory."

Jamie nodded. "I remember she helped me pick out Nora."

"Really?"

"She said Nora was the fattest puppy in Eureka."

Alison smiled. "I bet she was cute."

"Mommy said she looked like a butterball with feet."

"Did she?"

Jamie nodded slowly. His eyes filled with tears, and his lower lip trembled.

"She loved you very much," Alison whispered, "so much that she asked me before she . . . before she died to make sure that I took care of you. I am so very happy she asked me, because I love you too. She left me this house so you would have a warm place to sleep, and she left me some money so that you could have the things you need."

"Like my bike?" he mumbled.

"Like your bike."

For several seconds Jamie stared at her; then his face crumpled inward, and huge tears rolled down his cheeks. Alison took the mug from his hands and put her arms around him. He cried softly against her shoulder. She lifted him from the chair and rocked back and forth with him in her arms, kissing the soft cap of his hair, saying comforting words against his face.

He cried for several minutes, but eventually it subsided. She expected him to push away, but he didn't. He clung tight, his small arms circling her neck, his legs wrapped around her waist. Alison closed her eyes and held him.

Gradually a vague feeling of being watched stole over her, and she opened her eyes. Jack looked down at her. His eyes, behind his glasses, were dark. She opened her mouth, but he held a finger against her lips.

"He's asleep," Jack whispered. "Shall I carry him upstairs?"

"I will," Alison said. The two of them walked silently through the house. Jamie opened his eyes as Alison put him in his bed. She kissed his cheek and told him she loved him.

Jack followed her out into the hall. Alison leaned back against the wall, overcome with new feelings for Jamie and intensely aware of Jack. He put his palms flat against the wall on either side of her head and stared down at her in the dim light. He was so close, Alison could feel the warm stir of his breath on her forehead. She reached up and took his glasses from his face, folded them, and put them in his breast pocket. He leaned down slowly till his lips brushed hers.

"I like you very much," he whispered. She felt the formation of his words on her lips as much as she heard them. "I like you very, very much."

"I like you too," she said, caressing his cheek with shaky fingers.

"Is that all you feel for me?" Jack asked slowly.

Alison thought before she spoke. "It's too soon to tell," she replied, though she suspected it wasn't.

"Do you really think so?" he asked. He kissed her then. Alison felt the touch of his lips, the feel of his hand on the back of her neck, his closeness. She kissed him back, instinctively knowing that this kiss was the beginning for them.

"There's time," Jack said at length.

It always seemed to come down to that— time. "Yes," she agreed breathlessly.

He straightened up. She swallowed hard. "I'm going to go investigate the basement. Do you want to come?" she asked.

He shook his head and took a deep breath, his eyes never leaving hers. "I've got a new stack of books from the library to help with Grandfather's papers. Did Deanne tell you we're going to dinner at her house? Gram said she'd love to have Jamie for the evening."

"Wonderful," Alison said, abandoning all desire to cancel one moment with him.

He leaned down and kissed her again, a much briefer kiss, but no less intoxicating. He walked down the hall toward the light from his room. They exchanged one last long look before Alison turned to go downstairs.

The trunk was filled with clothes, but they were all old and yellowed. Alison used a knife and the flashlight to investigate the taped boxes. More clothes, most of them labeled with the name Rebecca Dawson. Some of the trunks held exquisite, silky gowns that Alison reluctantly decided to investigate further when the light was better. She stood and looked around the room. The windows were so dirty that little light could filter in, even in the middle of the day. On impulse she dashed upstairs for paper towels and glass cleaner and spent the next hour washing the insides of the windows.

Nora scratching at the top of the stairs reminded Alison how late it was getting. She put her things away, took Nora for a short walk before locking her in the garage, and went upstairs, eager to see Jack again.

His door was ajar, and the light was on. He was seated at his desk, but crumpled forward, his head resting on his arms, which lay over scattered papers and open books. His glasses were on the desk. One hand curled around an earpiece; the other was loosely wrapped around a broad black pen.

"Jack?" she whispered. He didn't answer or look up. Alison walked over to wake him so he could get into bed. For several seconds she stared at him, memorizing the way his hair curled slightly around his face, the angular cut of his jaw, the beautiful shape of his ear, the way his eyelashes lay like sooty smudges against his skin.

She reached down to shake his shoulder, but before her hand touched him, her gaze was caught by the single word written in bold black letters. It was the only visible word written in English. It was underlined three times, the last time so deeply it tore the lined paper.

Nadia, it said emphatically. Nadia.

Chapter Eight

*A*lison tried on everything in her closet before finally deciding on a copper-colored sweater and a pair of black silk slacks. She braided her hair, then took it out of the braid and twisted it into a French roll. She took the pins out and let her hair fall, brushing vigorously till it fell in soft waves to her shoulders. Was that too casual?

"This is what you get when you don't date much," she scolded her reflection. Her hands shook nervously as she tried to clasp the onyx necklace her mother had left her. She opened the door and called Jamie's name.

The little boy appeared almost at once, Nora on his heels.

"Would you help me with this?" Alison asked.

He nodded and followed her into her room. He didn't often come into the room, and Alison didn't know if it was because she was using it or his mother wasn't. She'd stored almost all of Mavis's personal possessions, and the room now reflected her taste, which was quieter, more traditional, and a lot less luxurious.

Jamie looked around, then climbed onto the bed. Alison sat down beside him, one hand holding her hair off her neck, the other fending off the dog, who seemed intent on rubbing against her legs. Alison thought the animal secretly delighted in leaving a trail of yellow hair on human clothing, the darker, the better.

With steady little fingers Jamie fastened the necklace.

"You're a peach," Alison told him.

He smiled at her and for once didn't lower his gaze as she looked at him closely. His cheeks had acquired a rosy glow since Jack had come to live with them.

She thought of the night earlier that week when she and Jack had kissed in the hallway. They'd avoided saying anything about it to each other, but the memory of his lips burned in her mind. Hard to believe it had been less than a month since he'd moved in. What in the world would she and Jamie do when Jack decided to rejoin the real world and teach again?

"There you guys are," Jack said from the

doorway. "We'd better get going. Gram is waiting with bated breath to see you, Jamie."

Jamie jumped off the bed and ran out of the room. Nora trotted after him. Alison rose more slowly. Jack was wearing dark-gray wool slacks, a white shirt, and a gray-and-cranberry cardigan. His dark hair was brushed back from his face. He looked every inch the young professor, his playful streak camouflaged by sedate clothing. Alison could hardly take her eyes off him.

"Do I pass inspection?" he asked her lightly.

She nodded slowly. "You look very nice."

"And you look delicious," he said suddenly. He held out his hand, and she took it.

Samantha Askarian met Jamie at her door. She was a comfortable woman, seventy years old, short and round, white hair pinned into a wild bun that dominated the top of her head. She was wearing a light-blue sweatshirt and matching sweatpants with a wide white stripe down each leg. She gathered Jamie like an armful of sun-dried laundry fresh from the line.

"How are you, honey? Wish you could have brought Nora, but my old sniffer blows up when dogs come around. How about you and me roasting hot dogs over the fire? Jack, you can start a small blaze in the fireplace, can't you?"

Alison wondered if he'd point out to his grandmother that he was hardly dressed for manual labor. He didn't. He just kissed her cheek and went out the back door, returning a few minutes later with an armload of kindling and a small log. Within minutes he had a little fire dancing and crackling on the grate.

"How is your translation of Leo's papers coming?" Jack's grandmother quizzed as he banked the log.

"Haven't had much time to work on it," Jack said.

Alison was sitting on the comfortable sofa, half her attention on Jamie as he talked to a sassy parakeet. When she heard Jack, she turned to look at him.

"I'm just so curious," the elderly woman said softly.

"I know, Gram. I've been teaching Jamie to ride a bike." Jack poked the fire and added, "Did Alison tell you I've been doing the cooking too?"

"You're very busy," Mrs. Askarian said slowly.

"Yes," Jack agreed. He poked at the log again and looked at Alison.

"Jack's a good cook," she said.

"As long as I don't get too fancy," Jack qualified.

"And he has been awfully busy lately. He's wonderful with Jamie, you know."

"Yes," Mrs. Askarian agreed. She sighed deeply as she glanced at her watch. "Hadn't you two better get along to your dinner date?"

"It's not really a date," Alison mumbled.

Jack laughed and took her arm, pulling her to her feet. "Calm down," he said gently. "We'll see you in a few hours, Gram."

"Have fun," Alison called to Jamie, but he was so involved with the green-and-yellow bird, she wasn't sure he heard.

"Why did you tell your grandmother you don't work on your grandfather's papers?" Alison asked Jack once they were back in the truck. She could still see the word "Nadia" etched into the paper. For four days she'd been eaten up with curiosity. Who was Nadia? "You're in there for hours every night, but if you need more time, I can take some of the work off your hands myself. For that matter, I would be happy to hire a cook and—"

"Honey, please. I just didn't want to tell Gram what I'm finding in those blasted papers, so I fed her a bunch of nonsense. I'm sorry. She caught me off guard."

Alison's insides turned to something approaching jelly at the endearment he threw her way with such ease. She didn't say anything as they drove to Deanne and Ben's house, content to sit in the old truck beside Jack, his arm just a touch away. He'd called her honey. She had every intention of getting to the bottom of what was bothering Jack, but she could wait till they were back home. This wasn't the right time to grill him. Besides, he'd called her honey.

Deanne and Ben lived in a small house set back in the redwoods. In the summer they entertained on the redwood deck that surrounded the back of the house. Alison had been there when raccoons came up to the deck to eat dog food Deanne left in a bowl for them. She'd seen deer nibble on their rosebushes. Tonight the yard was bathed in dark fog, and the living room seemed like an oasis of warmth and light.

Deanne greeted them at the door. She was wearing a long green caftan. Behind her, Ben's round smiling face resembled a moon. He wasn't yet forty, but his hair had receded, and he'd grown a short beard. He was the biggest man Alison knew, and he practically lifted her from the floor in greeting.

After introductions Deanne made sure everyone was comfortable around a low table covered with plates and bowls and trays of hors d'oeuvres. There were stuffed mushroom caps, tiny cheese quiches, shrimp wrapped in bacon, spicy warm meatballs, and sliced fresh vegetables with an herb dip.

"Do you want a job cooking for us?" Alison asked Deanne as she licked her fingers.

"Don't you cook like this?" Deanne asked Jack.

"Hardly," he said as he helped himself to another shrimp.

"Neither do I," she confessed. "Ben cooks."

"Whatever happened to traditional roles?" Jack asked, laughing. "You two beauties are the business tycoons, while Ben and I stay home cooking."

"Actually, I'm a commercial fisherman during salmon season," Ben said. "I cook only on weekends. 'Course, when the—"

"Ben!" Deanne squealed.

Ben's mouth snapped shut. He looked at Deanne sheepishly. "Sorry, hon. Didn't mean to steal your thunder."

Alison raised her eyebrows. "And what does that mean?"

Deanne smiled. "I told you I wanted you here for a reason. Ben honey, pass Jack one of those meatballs."

Alison laughed. "Deanne! What's going on?"

"Go on," Deanne insisted complacently, "take a meatball, Jack." Then she turned to Alison and blurted out, "I'm pregnant!"

Alison covered her mouth with her hands. "Oh, Deanne. You rascal, that's wonderful!"

"Yes," Deanne gushed. The two women hugged each other, and Jack shook Ben's hand. "I'm almost three months along and not a second of morning sickness! Isn't it great? We're so happy."

Ben scooted over closer to Deanne and swamped her thin shoulders with his arm.

Alison had only to observe the look Ben and Deanne exchanged to know how happy they were.

"And now for the bad news," Deanne said, interrupting Alison's musings.

"I'm not sure I can take any more news," Alison confessed.

"I'm going to have to take several months off work, maybe a year," Deanne said. "I want to have time with my baby, to bond with the little guy. I wouldn't mind working a few hours a day—heaven knows we could use the money—but we live so far out. I hate to leave right when you're moving the store, Ali, but I don't see how I can—"

Alison put her hand over Deanne's. "Stop now. The most important thing in the world

is your baby. You know that. We'll work something out when it's time for you to come back,
or I'll give you an extended maternity leave or
something."

"You've already done so much, what with
that raise," Ben said softly.

"It's only money," Alison said. "Imagine a
world where decisions were made because of
people, not money."

"Spoken like a wealthy woman," Jack
teased, but Alison felt him put his hand over
hers where it rested on the floor, and when she
looked at him, his eyes held the same expression she'd seen in the kitchen when he caught
her holding Jamie.

"This calls for champagne," Ben said as he
got to his feet.

"Orange juice for me," Deanne called out.
Then she looked at Alison and Jack and said,
"When are you two getting married?"

Alison immediately felt a flash fire rage on
her cheeks, and she practically choked on a
mushroom cap. She didn't dare look at Jack
and spared only a short "if looks could kill"
glance at Deanne. Jack squeezed her hand and
said, "We haven't gotten around to discussing
that yet."

Deanne laughed. "Me and my mouth again.
It's just the way you two look at each other. . . .

Okay, boss, I'll shut up. Here comes Ben with your champagne. Let's toast my baby!"

Later, as they drove home, a sleeping Jamie belted on the seat between them, Alison apologized for her friend's enthusiasm. "Deanne doesn't mean to put people on the spot," she said.

"Did she put you on the spot?" Jack asked without taking his gaze from the fog-shrouded street ahead of them.

"Yes, of course," Alison said. "We've known each other for only a few weeks."

"I feel as though I know you very well."

"I feel that way too," Alison agreed. "Still, asking us about marriage at this point is—well, it's absurd!"

"Of course." Jack's voice was light, and Alison could practically hear him grin. "Anyway, I wanted to explain about my grandfather's diary."

Alison put Deanne's embarrassing question out of her mind. "Great. You know I'm dying of curiosity."

"Yes. Well, it's simple, really. He was a young man in the early 1900s, and he kept a diary of sorts. Actually, as you've seen, it's an unruly batch of papers, all sizes and shapes, held together at one time by a folder of some sort. They're all loose now, and some of the dates are smeared. I tried to organize the mess before I began translating, and mostly I have, but there are still some gaps and holes, and things aren't entirely clear."

"Something is clear enough to make you uncomfortable about it, though," Alison said.

"Yes. Well, it seems to begin in 1913 when Leo was twelve and goes, off and on, until 1938. He left Russia in 1925. The Revolution was long over, and he was a young man. He was a married young man. . . ."

Jack's voice trailed off. Alison sat quietly. Jack had said his grandmother read no Russian, and besides, Samantha Askarian had to have been a child in 1925. At last Jack cleared his throat and continued.

"He left Russia and made his way here. I guess it took him several years. Anyway, eventually he met Gram and married her in 1936. She was only seventeen years old at the time."

"Women married young then," Alison said.

He didn't reply, and it was too dark in the truck to make out his features. Eventually he said, "My mother was born in 1938. Many, many times she told my brothers and me about her dad's escape from Russia and all his trials and tribulations as he made his way here. Gram told us too. It's the Askarian story, suitable for all occasions. Anyway, neither Gram nor my mother ever mentioned the Russian years, from 1913 to 1925. It seems strange, when you think about it, because the Revolution was in 1915 or so, and then Communism raised its ugly head. You'd have thought it would make quite an impact on Grandfather. They've never mentioned his having a wife, and they've never mentioned someone named Nadia."

"Nadia," Alison repeated softly.

Jack pulled the truck to a stop in the driveway. Jamie was leaning against Alison's arm. She brushed a straight dark lock from the child's forehead. "Nadia," Jack said. "Grandfather worshiped her. She was his child."

"And she died?" Alison asked.

Jack took his time answering. "I don't think so. I think Grandpa got up one morning and just left. He never went back. He never divorced Helena. And as far as I know, he never told a soul here about them. His marriage to my grandmother was a farce."

"But even if the marriage was valid in Russia, it may be that it wasn't valid here. . . . I suppose that's not the point, is it?"

Jack grunted. "No, it's not." He hit his fist on the steering wheel. "He was never married to Gram, Alison. How in the world do I tell her her beloved Leo abandoned one family? That means he never married her, not really. How do I tell her that?"

"Are you sure, Jack? Really sure there wasn't a divorce?"

"It's right there in his diary," Jack said firmly. "I quote, more or less: 'I kissed Helena good-bye this morning and then little Nadia. Will I ever see their sweet faces again?' Grandpa was something of a romantic."

Not if he left his wife and child, Alison decided. She said, "And then he left?"

"The next entry is two months later. He's in Finland, and he doesn't mention either of them. For that matter, he doesn't mention them again until his wedding day to Gram. Then he says something about Nadia."

"Not Helena?"

"Her too. Something about how painful it was to leave her behind and how he thought he'd never find happiness with a woman again." Jack sighed deeply and opened his door. "Well, now you know why I was evasive with Gram. I don't want to hurt her or her memory of Grandfather. I'm dying of curiosity about Nadia. I really don't know what to do."

"If I can help . . ." Alison said as Jack lifted Jamie. She didn't expect an answer, and she didn't get one. She unlocked the kitchen door

and led the way upstairs. Samantha Askarian
had put Jamie's pajamas on him at her house.
They took off his coat and slipped him into
bed. It wasn't until they were out in the hall
that Jack spoke again.

"Thanks, Alison, for listening."

"You're welcome," she said softly.

He leaned down and kissed her; then he
chuckled. "The idea of marrying me is absurd,
huh? I'll have you know I'm considered a heck
of a good catch."

"By all those brainy professor women or the
giggly coeds?" Alison joked softly.

"You'd be surprised," he said. He kissed her
again, and for a few minutes Alison forgot
about anything but him.

"You have the softest lips," Jack said at
length.

"Funny," she whispered, "I was just this
second thinking the very same thing about
you."

"Not as soft as yours," he insisted. He kissed
her again, several small kisses from the corner
of her mouth, across her eyelids, to her forehead. "You taste good too," he added.

"What do I taste like?"

"You taste like Alison Simmons, intrepid
girl flower designer."

"That's a surprise," she said, laughing softly.

"Speaking of surprises"—he straightened up—"you could have felled me with a feather when I heard that Courtney Howell was marrying someone other than Rob Polton. I had them both in a class last semester, and I would have bet money on their ending up happily ever after."

"I don't know if people ever do end up happily ever after," Alison said, smothering a yawn with one hand.

He kissed her nose. " 'Course they do. Good night, sweetheart. Sleep tight." With that, he opened her door and pushed her in, closing it softly behind her.

Chapter Nine

*T*he bike jamboree was unlike any event Alison had ever attended. Dozens of children, their bikes festooned with bright crepe-paper streamers and balloons, rode around the paved playground. The police had set up a booth and checked every bike with its small owner for safety features. Jamie proudly displayed his Safety First certificate, then careened off madly to join Brian and Tony in a race. Alison laughed aloud at his antics, hardly recognizing him as the quiet little boy so withdrawn only two months before.

The man responsible for the change, as far as Alison was concerned, put his arm casually around her shoulders. She liked the warm feel of his side against her, liked the smell of the fresh air and the sight of the sun that darted through the clouds every few minutes as though to promise that summer would eventually come to the North Coast.

"Your first grammar-school event?" Jack asked.

"Yes. I guess it's the first of many."

He smiled. "True. You kind of got kicked headfirst into this motherhood thing, didn't you?"

Alison nodded. She could see Jamie's bright-red jacket as he sped along on his bike. "Thanks to you, though, I'm getting the hang of it."

"You underestimate yourself," Jack said.

Alison smiled inwardly at the compliment. "Where are your parents and those little brothers?"

"Mom and Dad are back East. My brother Dave is a lawyer in Florida, and baby brother Joe is one of those child prodigies who know more about computers than their professors."

"And then there's you," Alison said softly.

"Right. I'm the underachiever in the family. I teach at a small university and take time off now and again for different projects or travel."

"Like your grandfather's diary. And us."

Jack looked down at her. "You and Jamie are different."

"Are we? I mean, sooner or later you'll go back to teaching, won't you?"

"This fall. I heard from the university a few days ago."

"I bet you're a wonderful teacher," Alison said sincerely.

"I try, just like you do," Jack said. "You and Jamie are getting closer, aren't you?"

"Yes, I think so," Alison agreed, remembering the way the child had actually brought a book into the den the night before and asked her to read it to him. Jack had been there, sitting at the desk, poring over his grandfather's diary, yet Jamie had asked her.

"Have you traveled much?" she asked Jack.

He shrugged. "A little now and again. Europe mostly. I don't have a big savings account, probably never will."

"Me too," Alison agreed without thinking.

Jack laughed. "You? You're one of the richest women in Humboldt County!"

"Oh, that. That's not my money. Mavis accumulated that. I just try not to let it ruin my life."

He shook his head. "Honey, whether you like it or not, you are rich."

"Does that matter?" Alison asked quietly.

He didn't say anything for several minutes, and when he did, it was about Jamie. "Look! He beat Tony, of all things. Let's go down and congratulate him."

"You go ahead," Alison called as Jack ran off down the field. She pulled her coat closer around her, wondering if his lack of response meant anything.

They didn't get back to the house till well after two in the afternoon. Grace, who hadn't reported in for work that morning, was sitting on the kitchen steps, her back hunched, her arms trailing between her legs. An old suitcase sat on the ground by her feet along with a potted African violet and a sleeping bag. She looked up slowly when she heard the truck.

"Grace?" Alison asked. "Are you okay?"

"No!" she cried; then the tears started flowing down her face. By the look of her bloodshot eyes and red nose, they weren't the first tears of the day. For once she wasn't wearing the obligatory jumper and blouse but a tattered pair of jeans and a sweater three sizes too large that she'd stretched over her knees. She produced a small package of tissues from the folds of her sweater and blew her nose.

Alison sat down on the step beside her. "What is it, Grace? Are you hurt?"

"It's Danny," she wailed.

"Her husband," Jack contributed.

"He—he left," Grace stuttered. "And I'm going to have a baby, and he couldn't care less."

A baby! Was everybody pregnant? "I'm sure he does," Alison said.

Jack was leaning over them, unlocking the door. "Help me get her inside, Alison, where it's warm. Jamie, grab the flower, will you, sport?"

"Not my plant!" Grace wailed. "Don't break my plant."

Jamie handed the plant to Grace who clutched it to her as though it were her last friend in the world. Alison picked up the sleeping bag.

They got Grace and her meager possessions inside the warm kitchen. "Take Grace's suitcase up to the bedroom next to yours, will you, honey?" Alison asked Jamie, who dragged the big bag out of the room. Seconds later they all heard it thumping up the stairs. Alison put on a pot of water. Jack sat down beside Grace and took one of her icy-cold hands into his.

"Can you tell us about it?" he asked gently.

Grace stopped crying long enough to blow her nose again and say, "I guess so."

Alison sat down across from Jack and waited. She knew he'd have Grace talking faster than she ever could. At last Grace wiped her eyes with a fresh tissue and set the African violet on the table in front of her.

"Danny came home late last night. I was already in bed. I get tired easily now—you know how it is."

"How far along are you?" Alison asked.

"Four months. Didn't you know?"

Alison shook her head, thinking that at least the ill-fitting jumper was explained.

"Potter knew," Grace said. "I thought sure she told you. Anyway, Danny wanted to know where his dinner was, and I said if he couldn't get home on time or at least call, then he could fix his own dinner." Her voice petered out as a new set of tears made their way down the shiny trail left by the previous set.

"He started yelling at me. He said I was a—a lousy housekeeper and an awful cook, which is true, but he didn't need to shout it at me. He said I was a nag and that he never wanted to see me again. Oh, Miss Simmons, Mr. Foxx, I don't know what to do!" The recital ended in a new spasm of sobs.

"You can stay here as long as you like," Alison assured her.

"Danny will be back," Jack said so matter-of-factly that even Alison looked at him. The effect on Grace was galvanizing.

"Do you really think so?"

"Of course. He's probably just tired from working long hours and nervous about becoming a father. I bet he's taking out his own frustrations on you."

"That would be just like him," Grace admitted without contempt. "I hope he comes back, Mr. Foxx."

"Jack, remember?"

"Yeah."

"Let's go upstairs," Alison prompted, "and get you settled in. There, the tea kettle is whistling. I'll make you a hot cup of herbal tea."

"That would be . . . nice," Grace mumbled.

"You help Grace; I'll make the tea," Jack suggested.

An hour later Alison sank down onto the chair across from Jack. Grace was comfortably ensconced upstairs in the frilly room reserved for female nannies, a box of tissues at one elbow, a cup of steaming tea at the other, the African violet safely placed on the dresser. Alison had the feeling Grace would fall asleep soon—she looked exhausted.

"You look a little tuckered out yourself," Jack told Alison.

"Not me! I have a meeting with Mr. Morgan in half an hour to sign more papers for the new building, and then I want to go back to work for a couple of hours."

"You're a dynamo, aren't you?"

She smiled. "I want to get a load from the

storeroom over the shop. Remember, I showed it to you one day? I figured out the other morning that if I take one load a day, I'll have the place emptied by the time our lease is up."

"Where are you going to put all that junk?"

"I beg your pardon?" she snarled playfully.

"Oh, sorry. Where are you going to store all those priceless floral relics?" He took a sip of tea and added, "The new building?"

"That's better. No, not there. It's scheduled to be painted next week. I'll bring everything here. There's always a corner of the basement."

"Just honk when you get here," Jack said, "and Jamie and I will help you unload."

Alison stood wearily. Jack was right; she was tired. She hadn't been sleeping well lately. She kept thinking about Nadia. For the past week Jack had been scouring the diary, looking for anything he might have missed that would help him explain to his grandmother why her husband had never divorced his first wife.

Several times Jack had read short passages aloud. The young man exposed by those inner thoughts had been sensitive, kind. Being a few years too young to fight in the Revolution, he'd nonetheless agonized over the despair and suffering of his countrymen. And when he met Helena, his life had blossomed. Nadia's birth a year later was almost too much joy. And then two years later he'd walked away from them. It didn't make any sense. Alison couldn't believe it had happened that way, and she hadn't even known the man.

She was back three hours later with a vanload of everything from Halloween decorations to silk poinsettias, dried roses to three cases of green glass vases that hadn't sold well. She honked the horn as Deanne's car pulled into the driveway behind her.

"You didn't need to come," Alison told Deanne. "Jack and Jamie will help me unload."

"I want to see those boxes of clothes you told me about," Deanne said. Jack opened the outside basement door from the inside and propped it open. Nora burst forth like champagne from a shaken bottle, delighted to see Alison, delighted to see Deanne, delighted period.

"Hi, Aunt Deanne," Jamie said. He'd followed Nora outside, a little more quietly. He slipped his hand into Alison's. She tried to look as though it were no big deal, while her heart did flip-flops in her chest.

"Hello, handsome," Deanne said. She plucked a red carnation from her hair and stuck it in one of Jamie's buttonholes.

Jack had opened the back of the van. He pulled out a huge jack-o-lantern man complete with accordion legs and arms, and he laughed.

"Three years ago, right?" Deanne asked Alison. "Remember? We propped him up in a corner with about three dozen orange mums and a hundred black carnations."

"Must have been lovely," Jack said dryly.

"Looked like a homecoming float," Deanne told him with a wink. "And the boss made us dress up in costumes."

"That's enough," Alison scolded. "I don't need editorial remarks. You two he-men unload this van while I show the lady some old motheaten clothes. Come on, Deanne."

It was the first time Alison had been downstairs since she'd washed the inside of the windows. She was amazed by the light that poured through the streaked glass. While she searched for the right place to store things from the shop, Deanne started in on the trunks.

Squeals of delight brought Alison from the dark corners back to the center of the main room. Deanne was down on her knees. She'd spread the contents of several trunks on their lids. Alison was startled by the rich colors—velvety red, peach satin, sapphire blue. Deanne had opened one of the trunks that Alison hadn't investigated.

"They're wonderful," Deanne gushed. "They're marvelous. Oh, Alison, what a find!" She looked at a label sewn into the neck of a particularly rich ivory gown. "Who's this Rebecca Dawson?"

"Former owners of the house," Grace said from halfway down the inside stairs. Her face wasn't as puffy, but her eyes were rimmed with deep, dark circles, and her voice sounded faded, wilted. "Jenny Dawson owned the place for fifty years before Mrs. Dufour bought it," Grace continued as she reached the basement floor. "Rebecca Dawson was her mother."

Both Alison and Deanne had turned to stare at Grace. She was back in her jumper, her pregnancy obvious now that Alison knew about it. Grace joined them.

"How could they have stayed in such good condition down here all that time?" Deanne mused aloud.

"They weren't down here except for the last few months, since Mrs. Dufour had that automobile accident and died," Grace said. "Mrs. Dufour kept them in the room Mr. Foxx—Jack, that is—is using."

"Then how did they end up down here?" Deanne asked.

"Potter," Grace said bitterly. "As soon as Mrs. Dufour died, she had me haul all this 'trash' down here. "Said it 'smelled' and she didn't want to have it in the house. Well, Mr. Morgan had told me to obey Mrs. Potter, so

I did what she asked, but it really made me mad."

"This was before I moved in?" Alison asked.

"Right before. Mrs. Potter took over, just like that. Fired that nice girl Gretchen who took such good care of the little boy. I was sure glad when you got here, Alison. Jamie is looking happy again, thanks to you. And Jack."

Alison smiled her thanks, her gaze fastened on Deanne as she flitted from trunk to trunk, excited exclamations of pleasure escaping her lips. "Wouldn't it be fun to have a Victorian Day at the shop?" Deanne asked at last. "You and I and Chris could all dress up in these gowns, and we could push pink roses and lilacs and larkspur—you know, old-fashioned kinds of flowers. I wonder if any of these dresses are big enough around the middle for me. I swear, I've gained ten pounds already, and it's all crouching here on my waist like a giant inner tube."

Alison looked at her friend's slender figure and shook her head. Deanne laughed. "Trust me; it's there." She looked at Grace, and her eyes widened. "Are you expecting too, Grace? That's wonderful! I bet you and your husband are as delighted as Ben and I are."

Grace smiled shakily. "Yes," she said, her gaze down on her feet and her voice trembling.

To divert unwanted attention away from Grace, Alison held up an emerald-green gown with velvet trim. "What do you think?"

Grace swallowed hard. She seemed determined to keep her composure, and Alison admired her for it. Grace wrinkled her brow and looked through the other dresses, choosing at last a delicate pink dress with an opalescent shimmer. She handed it to Alison. "With your coloring, this one's better."

Deanne took the green dress, while Alison took off her coat and slipped the pink one over her head. It was big enough to fit over her clothing. Deanne fastened the back of the dress as Jack and Jamie brought down their third load.

Alison didn't see them. She twirled around once. The full skirt rustled and shimmered. She stopped to laugh and found herself face-to-face with Jack.

"Beautiful," he said softly.

Alison suddenly felt as though she and Jack were alone in a flashback scene from an old movie. His eyes were dark and soft, drowning pools of liquid umber. She yearned to touch him, throw herself into his arms, dance around the basement while an invisible orchestra struck up a waltz and Jack held her close against him.

Deanne's laughter broke the split-second spell. "Have you asked her yet?" she asked.

Jack smiled slowly. "Not yet," he said, never taking his eyes from Alison's face.

"Asked her what?" Jamie demanded.

"If she loves me," Jack said.

Alison gasped. Jamie said, " 'Course she does. She loves both you and me. Don't you, Alison?"

Alison looked down at the small upturned face and touched his nose with her finger. "Yes," she said softly. "Yes, I do."

He grinned at her, then demanded to know where he was supposed to put the bag of ribbon scraps he was carrying. Alison pointed at a corner, glared at Deanne for once again putting Jack in an awkward position, and with Grace's help took off the pink dress.

Deanne took four dresses home with her that evening to drop off at the cleaner's on her her way to work the next morning. Long after everything from the van had been stored and Jack was upstairs starting dinner, Alison lingered in the basement, carefully storing the dresses back in their trunks. She liked the feel of the big room. She liked the narrow horizontal windows and the wide-open space. She even liked the out-of-the-way corners and the broad stairs that led up to the outside.

She sat down on one of the trunks, a fragile, pale-blue taffeta dress in her lap. For a while she thought about the shop and the gearing up for the Easter rush that was due to start the next day. Sam would deliver scads of Easter lilies and tulips. Maybe she should order extra daffodils and irises from the local bulb farm. She'd have to call Mary Rosewater and arrange for her farm to deliver ten or twelve bunches of each. Bulb flowers were always big sellers in the spring. Let's see . . . Mary's number was downstairs in the shop.

Alison bit at her lip. What in the world was she thinking about? For a second there she'd been back in her other life, some four months before, upstairs in her apartment over the shop. Boy, had that living arrangement been handy! Many nights she'd stayed up till all hours poring over the books or getting a head start on the next day's work, knowing all the while that all she had to do was climb the stairs to go to bed.

The floor overhead creaked as Jack walked from one end of the kitchen to the other. Alison listened carefully. She could hear a high voice, probably Jamie's, and then a muffled bark. She fingered the crisp taffeta as she smiled to herself, content to hear them moving and speaking above her. The water pipes overhead rumbled and complained.

The taffeta was crisp and cool. Deanne was right; dressing in the gowns for a couple of days would be fun. Too bad it couldn't be in this old house where the antique dresses matched the graceful old structure.

Maybe it was the feel of the fabric in her hands, the thought of the shop, the sight of the shop's discards in one corner, the sounds of the house above her, and the slight aroma of chicken wafting down from the kitchen. All at once the focus switched, the kaleidoscope turned, all the variables condensed into one glorious idea that leaped into her mind with a physical jolt.

Two Hearts Florist could move to this very basement! Why not?

What about zoning laws? her practical self asked.

What about them? the romantic answered.

Alison stood abruptly. She opened the trunk and gently stored the dress, then closed the trunk. The house was so close to downtown. A woman across the street operated a beauty salon in her sitting room. And how about the man three doors down who advertised his homemade redwood patio furniture in the newspaper?

She plopped back down on the trunk. Her heart was hammering on the walls of her chest, either from excitement or nerves or a combination of both. The hairs on her arms stood upright, sensitized as she rolled the idea of moving the shop into the basement over and over in her head.

"Well, why not?" she said aloud.

Because this is Mavis's house.

That one stopped her for only a second. "It's my house. Mine and Jamie's," she announced.

You can't raise a kid like Jamie in a place over a florist shop.

You call a three-story mansion a place above a shop? What does he care what's in the basement? This way you'd be here for him, all the time. All he'd have to do is come downstairs. Jack can't stay here taking care of Jamie forever, you know. He's going back to the university, and you're going to have to replace him, impossible as that may seem.

What in the world will Mr. Morgan say?

Probably a lot. But so what? He's your lawyer; he'll do what you want.

What about the papers you just signed on the other building?

What about them? Cancel the deal. If it's too late, instruct Lucy Van Ness to sell it.

Which brings us to the last point. What about

your precious independence? What about your oath not to let Mavis's money change your life? What about all the times you told yourself and everyone else that Mavis's money wasn't going to be used on your business?

This one stumped Alison for a few minutes. She thought of Jamie and Grace, who depended on her. Mavis had wanted the inheritance to be used to assure Jamie a happy, safe childhood. Two Hearts Florist was Alison's way of doing just that. In her mind's eye she saw her flamboyant cousin laughing at all the silly inner dialogue, and in that instant Alison made up her mind.

For an hour Alison walked around the big room. It had its own outside entrance. It had water and plumbing. Ideas tumbled over one another. She looked at the floor and saw oak parquet, looked at the walls and envisioned airy wallpaper, looked at the exposed pipes on the ceiling and saw bright white paint, beams, and ceiling fans. It could be, it would be, beautiful!

Chapter Ten

*T*he days ahead were filled with decisions to be made amid the overpoweringly sweet smell of Easter lilies. Jack had pronounced her idea "Terrific!" Mr. Morgan had rubbed his eyes and, shaking his head, had agreed to look into zoning laws and such. Lucy Van Ness had promptly put the new property back on the market without saying a word other than pressing the name of a good contractor on Alison.

"And I'll miss all the fun," Deanne said. It was Thursday morning, and they were helping Sam unload his delivery van. Eight dozen red roses, two dozen, each, white, pink, yellow, and peach roses, dozens of tulips, daffodils, irises, carnations, fresias, football mums, and gladiolus, to say nothing of the dozens of stems of ferns, winter bud, huckleberry, eucalyptus, and baby's breath.

153

There were also paper-wrapped pots of philodendrons, African violets, tulips, azaleas, and chrysanthemums. Shirley and Chris began the long process of preparing the flowers for use, clipping each stem, wiring the head of each rose, carefully propping each in a tall bucket of cool water mixed with floral preservative.

Alison walked Sam to his van, pausing to sign the delivery form.

"I'll check into the lilac thing," Sam said as he pulled himself up into the van. He grinned and added, "Imagine some little girl wanting lilacs in December."

"The customer is always right," Alison mused. "Anyway, next week I think you'd better bring an extra box of orchids. We always end up making lots of corsages around this time of year."

He made a note on his clipboard. "I'm going to San Francisco to the Flower Market myself," he said. "See you next week, Ali."

Alison waved good-bye and went back into the shop. The workroom was crowded with flowers, the fragrance heady and full.

Deanne was on the phone, and she motioned Alison over, her face twisting into a clown expression as she handed Alison the receiver.

"Hello?"

"Alison?"

It was Courtney Howell's voice. "Hi," Alison said. "I was just talking to my flower distributor about your lilacs. He didn't know offhand if he can get them, but—"

"That's just it," Courtney interrupted. "There's been another change of plans. Barton and I were talking it over, and we decided the wedding should be more elegant."

"Fine," Alison said, though she thought the word "elegant" had to have come from Mrs. Howell. "What do you have in mind?"

"All white," Courtney said hesitantly. "White everything."

"I did a wedding like that a year or two ago," Alison said. "It was exquisite."

"Really?"

"Yes. We used stephanotis and scads of white rosebuds. The bride wore a Juliet cap of baby roses and baby's breath—it was heavenly. With your coloring, you'll be absolutely gorgeous. And, Courtney, just about any flower you can imagine comes in white, and we can get them all in the middle of winter."

"You make it sound lovely," Courtney said slowly.

"I guarantee it. If you still want those baskets, we can fill them with white snapdragons, pom-pom mums, carnations, roses, fresias, gladiolus—see what I mean? You'll love it."

"Mother . . . Barton will be thrilled."

"And you?" Alison asked for some reason.

"Of course!" Courtney agreed, but there was a false note of bravado in her voice.

Alison felt sorry for her. She wished she could advise her to wait till she was sure. But maybe there wasn't a problem at all. After all, how well did she know Courtney Howell?

"I'll drop by with new scraps of fabric in the next week or two," Courtney told her. "And I meant to tell you how cute your little boy is."

"Thank you," Alison said. "I'm pretty partial to him myself."

"Did I understand right? Professor Foxx is baby-sitting him for you?"

"Sort of," Alison evaded.

Courtney sighed. "I see. Well, see you soon. Thanks for being so patient with me."

Alison hung up the phone thoughtfully. Deanne thrust an order for a dozen red roses into her idle hands, and she was off and running again.

It was late when Alison left for the day, but although she was tired from a day full of flowers and phone calls, she felt the now-familiar rush of anticipation at seeing Jamie and Jack again. Besides, she'd had a strange call from

Samantha Askarian that afternoon, one that made her feel uneasy.

"You tell that boy that Leo Askarian was my husband and I want to know what all that Russian means," Jack's grandmother had scolded. "I saw that stack of papers, Alison, and I know hedging when I see it. Jack's keeping something from me, and I want to know what it is."

When Alison made some sort of noncommittal noise, Samantha snorted. "I'd be willing to put good money on the fact that he's dug up something unpleasant and that he's told you about it. I know the boy's crazy about you. That's why I'm going over his head, woman to woman. Now, I'm not going to ask you to divulge a confidence, but you will talk to him for me, won't you?" Alison had promised she would.

Grace was in the kitchen. A delicious smell rose with the steam from a big pot on the stove that Grace was stirring.

"Soup," Grace said. "Don't worry, Alison. Jack put it on before he left."

Jamie and Nora ran into the kitchen. The child wrapped an arm around Alison's leg as he demanded to know if she remembered where he'd put his miniature cars. Nora detoured to the stove to sniff the air. The dog recognized vegetable-beef soup when she smelled it.

"Second shelf above your bed," Alison told Jamie. She opened the refrigerator and took out a diet root beer. "You said Jack left?" she asked Grace as Jamie and Nora disappeared out the door.

"He got all excited about something today while Jamie was in school. He was pacing the hall, waiting for you to get home. I offered to watch Jamie so he could leave, he was that anxious to get somewhere." Grace put the lid back on the pot and set the spoon down in a bowl to keep the rich brown broth from staining the drainboard. "I don't know why people don't trust me with that child," Grace added. She looked up at Alison quickly. "I really do like the little guy."

"I know you do," Alison assured her. She wasn't quite sure what the housekeeper was alluding to. "And I trust you with Jamie. Who doesn't?"

"Potter," Grace snarled. "And Mrs. Dufour. She liked foreign nannies. Potter didn't like anyone." Grace sat down opposite the chair where Alison had plopped to take off her shoes and rub her feet. "I offered to watch him, you know. I couldn't understand why Mrs.

Dufour had to have someone from Norway or Spain or even France once."

Alison thought she did. A nanny from France sounded a lot more sophisticated than a nanny from down the street. Besides, Grace had other obligations and couldn't live at the house all the time. Mavis had traveled so extensively, she needed someone for Jamie who was here twenty-four hours a day.

"Would you like to take charge of Jamie after Jack leaves?" Alison asked suddenly. "I wouldn't need you at night, so you'd be free to go back home to Danny."

Grace's face fell. "Oh, I am sorry," Alison cried. She put her hand on Grace's arm. "I didn't mean—"

"I know, I know," Grace assured her. "Sometimes I forget myself. Sometimes I get to thinking I'd better get on home and start dinner for Danny. You know, a sandwich or a can of soup or something."

Alison knew. Maybe she and Grace could take cooking classes together that summer. "Anyway," Alison continued, her voice cheerful, "I would love it if you could watch Jamie here at the house on the weekdays after school and during the summer. I'll be right downstairs, you know. Oh, that reminds me, the contractor Lucy Van Ness told me about is due here any minute."

"What about nights and weekends?" Grace asked.

"I'll be here," Alison said and couldn't help wondering, would Jack?

"I'll have the baby by then, you know. What would I do with it?"

"You'd bring him or her, of course. We have so many rooms in this house. How about Mrs. Potter's room on the ground floor? It could be your nursery away from home."

Grace winced again.

"Danny will come back," Alison said firmly. "Remember what Jack said? Is he ever wrong?"

"No," Grace agreed. "I'd love to continue working here. I can't think of anywhere else where I could have my baby with me all day. And I told you how I feel about Jamie."

Alison and Grace shook hands. Alison felt as though a huge weight had been lifted from her heart. She had only a second to wonder why Jack had been so anxious to rush out. She wanted to tell him about his grandmother's call. A rap on the kitchen door interrupted her thoughts.

"Name's Petersen," a young man announced. He was clad in blue jeans and a red down vest over a blue-and-green plaid shirt. Alison knew he was the contractor because of his name, but his tanned face would have been a sure giveaway by itself. It took concentrated effort, a tanning salon, or an outside job to get a tan in April in Northern California.

Alison slipped on her shoes and rose to shake hands and introduce herself and Grace. Then she opened the basement door, switched on the light, and led him down to the basement.

"This is really neat," Lon Petersen said half a dozen times as he stalked around the basement. He listened to her as she explained what she wanted, but didn't take any notes. Alison thought he couldn't be much older than she was, but Lucy Van Ness had recommended him. "He's good and he's fast," she'd said.

"But do you understand what I want?" Alison asked him.

"Sure. You want a room here where the stairs come down. It will be your delivery entrance. You want another door over here"—he took long strides toward the front of the house—"as the main entrance. A room here will be the showroom. You need storage rooms over there, electricity, a ceiling, good lighting, a wood floor, water piped in here and here and here. And you want a bathroom over there."

He stomped hard on the concrete floor, apparently found it suitable, and added, "And you want a parking area created out in the side yard."

He'd pointed in all the right directions at the right times. Alison smiled. "Yes. Can you do it?"

"Sure. Did you check zoning laws and building permits and all that?"

"My lawyer is doing it."

"No problem," Petersen said with a grin. "I can have it done for you in a month if we put a rush on it, two if we don't."

"Take your time and do it right," Alison told him.

"I'll send you a written estimate next week," he said. "Or should I send it to that lawyer you mentioned?"

"Send it here, please," Alison said and shook his hand.

She and Jamie and Grace ate dinner alone that evening. Jack didn't come; he didn't call. Alison got a small taste of what life was going to be without him and didn't like it one bit. She and Jamie and Jack were a family. She'd had her hesitations, and he'd had his, but it was time they talked them out.

*   *   *

Everyone was in bed, even Nora, when Alison finally heard the front door open and close. She got out of bed, put on her robe and belted it tightly around her waist. She had a promise to keep to Samantha Askarian, but first she needed to talk to Jack about the two of them.

She met him in the hallway where they usually held their midnight chats. This thought brought a smile to Alison's lips.

"Boy, is it good to come home to you!" Jack said. He reached out an arm to hug her.

"You're damp," she said. "Is it raining outside?"

"Misting heavily." He released her and took off his jacket.

"I have to talk to you," Alison said. "Shall we go to the kitchen and have a cup of coffee?"

"Actually, I think I'll heat up a bowl of soup. Didn't get around to eating dinner tonight."

He hung his jacket on his doorknob before they went downstairs. Alison convinced Jack that even she could reheat soup. He sat at the table watching her. He looked tired. "The boss isn't supposed to fix the nanny dinner," he said playfully.

Alison plopped down on his lap. He wrapped his arms around her waist. "I'm not your boss, and you know it," she said as she kissed him on the tip of his nose.

"You signed my check last month," he pointed out.

"Yes. I don't want to sign any more."

"Am I fired?" he asked.

"Hardly. It's just that you and I . . . it's just that Jamie and you. . . ."

"My soup is burning," Jack said, smiling.

"Oh!" Alison sprang to her feet and took the pan off the burner. She poured some of the soup into a bowl, snatched a package of crackers from the pantry, and set it all in front of Jack. It felt nice to wait on him for a change.

He pulled her back onto his lap.

"Your soup will get cold," she warned.

"My soup won't get cold till a week from next Wednesday. Besides, you were in the middle of tying your tongue in knots."

Alison took a deep breath. She didn't know where to begin. She looked into his eyes, and then she did know.

"I love you," she said. "I love you, I love you, I love you."

"I love you too," Jack said, laughing. Somehow it wasn't the tender, romantic moment Alison had imagined, but it was right, nonetheless. He kissed her soundly on the lips and added, "Go on—"

"Jack, you know darn good and well what I'm trying to say. You're just having a good time watching me make a big fool of myself."

He took both her hands into his and squeezed them tight. "I have nothing to offer," he said softly. "I'm almost penniless. I aspire to be nothing but a decent teacher. I love you Alison, but—"

Alison stopped his words by planting her lips on his. She kissed him until she could feel him abandon his speech. Then she pulled away and said, "Professor Foxx, don't be an idiot."

He stared at her long and hard. At last he opened his mouth. "Miss Simmons, I love you with all my heart. I love Jamie too. I even love that gold hair ball, Nora. I want to take care of the three of you forever, even though I realize you can take care of yourself and the rest of this menagerie perfectly well without me. The truth of the matter is that I need you, and I think you need me. I want to be a part of your life."

Alison kissed his forehead. "Don't you know, Jack? You are my life."

"Is there someone I should ask for your hand? Your father, maybe?" Jack asked. His voice was husky.

"He's too busy reeling in salmon," Alison managed to squeak.

Again he stared at her. Finally he took a deep breath and said, "Will you marry me?"

She flung her arms around his neck. "Yes, yes, yes—"

It wasn't till they'd sealed their engagement with a prolonged kiss that Alison paused to wonder about Jamie. What would he think?

Chapter Eleven

"We'll tell Jamie after we make all the plans," Jack said at last. He kissed both her cheeks. "And Grace, though the poor woman will undoubtedly break into tears. She misses that Danny of hers."

The bowl of soup was cold and untouched. Alison sighed heavily and rested her head against Jack's shoulder. She could feel his heart thump under her cheek and would have been content to stay right there on his lap in the kitchen for the rest of her life.

Then she remembered her promise and sat up abruptly. "Jack! I almost forgot. Your grandmother called today. She's desperate to know what you've found. You've got to talk to her, honey."

He put her fingers to his lips and kissed them. "I did. Tonight."

"Good," Alison said slowly. "How did she take it?"

"Heat up my soup and let me tell you about my day," Jack said.

Alison stood and dumped the bowl of soup back into the pan. She turned the heat on low and stood with her back to the stove. "Okay, shoot."

"I was reading through that pile of papers again today," he began, "when I ran across a name. I had seen it before, of course, but since it had obviously been written down recently, more or less, I didn't pay it much attention."

"How did you know it was recent?"

"The ink. The only non-faded ink on any of the papers. Anyway, it was a Russian name, and something about it bothered me. I finally realized the surname was the same as one of Grandfather's friends, one of the boys he wrote a lot about way back when. I double-checked the two names, and sure enough, they were the same and they both lived in Leningrad. Nicolas and Alexi Paszitnov."

Alison stirred the soup and poured it into the bowl again. Jack tasted it carefully and grinned. "I'm turning into a pretty good cook, aren't I?" he asked. "Made the beef stock myself with some scraps from a roast and a package of—"

"Jack!"

"Okay. Anyway, the neat part is that there was a telephone number with the recent entry."

"Don't tell me it was his phone number!"

"Not exactly. I guess not everyone there has a phone, like we do. But it was the number of a friend of a friend, and I left a message that I'd call back in two hours. I'll owe you a few dollars on the next telephone bill, by the way."

"I think we can work it out," Alison said.

"Right. Anyway, I finally got hold of him this afternoon, though it was either yesterday or tomorrow there—I couldn't be sure."

"He's a friend of your grandfather's?"

"Son of a friend. Nicolas, the old man, died two years ago. The son, Alexi, is a nice guy. I know Russian, and he knew a little English, so we got along fine. The thing is, Alison, Grandfather tried to keep in touch with Nicolas. Of course, until recently, until this new open-door policy and Glasnost, it was only a matter of smuggled letters every few years through mutual friends. But apparently, a few months before Grandfather died, he arranged a call and spoke with Alexi."

"About what?" Alison asked. She poured a little more soup into Jack's bowl and sat across from him at the table.

"By then Grandfather was dying. I gather he had to know, really know, about the people he left behind."

"Helena!"

"No. Helena died the day before Grandfather left. Her parents took Nadia and moved to Moscow. Politically they were a world apart from Grandfather, and they told him that he wouldn't see the child again. He had no reason to doubt them. I gather he buried Helena and lost Nadia on the same awful day in 1925."

"And so he kissed them both good-bye and wondered if he'd ever see them again."

"One in heaven, the other on earth," Jack said softly. "I suppose he planned on returning for Nadia, but it was impossible. With the political climate now, he might have been able to visit, but he was failing in health for several years, and then, of course, he'd never told Gram any of this. But he never forgot Nadia."

"Does Nadia know about him?"

"No."

"And your grandmother knew nothing?"

"She knew he'd undergone a great tragedy back in Russia, but she didn't know what, and he wouldn't talk about it." Jack finished off his soup and added, "I gave her Alexi's address and the phone number this afternoon. She can write or call and find out more when she's ready. For now, she's so relieved her Leo didn't have another family in Reno, she's willing to overlook a lot.''

"That's wonderful," Alison said.

"Yes," Jack agreed. "Now tell your fiancé about your day, my love. How's the redecorating going?''

Alison smiled before she told him about Lon Petersen, reflecting that this was the first of a lifetime of evenings when they would share the day's events, basking in the love and security of each other.

As to be expected, Deanne was beside herself when Alison announced her engagement at the shop the next morning. "I knew it, I knew it!" she cried, embracing Alison tightly.

"Yes, you did," Alison agreed. The two women exchanged deep, satisfied smiles till Deanne gestured at the dresses she'd picked up from the cleaner's on her way to work. They were hanging over the door, their shimmering jewel-tone colors as vibrant as the day they were sewn.

"Ali, I have a wonderful idea! Why don't you get married in one of these gowns? This ivory one, for instance. Oh, look, it's perfect!''

Alison held the ivory satin and lace beneath her chin and looked in the tiny mirror fastened to the back of the door. The fabric was soft and silky to the touch. "It's beautiful," she agreed. "What a great idea! And you, as my matron of honor, can wear one too."

"Yes," Deanne said softly. "We'll have to have our old-fashioned day here at the shop pretty soon," she added. "I don't want to miss it. I think this blue one will still get around me."

"I'm sure it will, but I think we should save the dresses for the opening of the shop at its new location. It'll take about two months to complete the renovation of the basement. We're getting married very soon, but we're saving our honeymoon till Jamie is out of school. Jack has some money saved, and he wants to take us to Hawaii. Mr. Morgan informed me recently that Mavis owned a small house on Maui, so we'll go there. It's Jamie's now, so we'll take the little land baron with us."

Deanne smiled, but her eyes were bright with tears. "I know it's silly. I just wanted to be part of the dress thing. I love this stupid shop, and as much as I want my baby, I want this job too, and I can't have both. Never mind me, Ali. Pregnancy has reduced me to a quivering Jell-O mold. I swear, I cry at the drop of a hat."

"I've been thinking," Alison said softly.

"Grace is going to have her baby about a month before yours is due. She and I are going to fix up one of the rooms in the house as a nursery; then she's going to watch Jamie afternoons. Why couldn't she watch your baby too, once you're ready to return?"

"Would she?" Deanne asked, her eyes lighting up.

"I think so. If it's too much work, we'll hire more help. Who knows? One of these days I might have a baby too."

"But can you hold my job open six months?"

"Sure. Chris is already learning how to arrange. We'll move her back here with Shirley and me and hire someone for the front. What do you think?"

Deanne opened her mouth, snapped it shut, and dissolved into tears. She bit her lip and nodded furiously.

"I think she likes the idea," Chris observed from the doorway.

The wind came up that afternoon. Alison tied a scarf around her head and walked against it to the house, glad for the time alone to think. She and Jack still hadn't told Jamie or Samantha about their engagement, and while she was looking forward to the expressions on their faces, she was a tiny bit hesitant too. Not about Samantha. She knew Jack's grandmother would be ecstatic and had the sneaking suspicion she wouldn't even be surprised. But she was still worried about Jamie and how he would take the news.

Jack prepared one of his specialties—hamburgers. He had Jamie lock Nora in the garage, and he and Grace scrubbed the kitchen till it shone, but more important, till there wasn't a dog hair to be seen—or sniffed—because Samantha was coming to dinner.

Samantha Askarian arrived with a bouquet of pink camellias. "Trust me to bring flowers to a florist," she said as she handed the flowers to Alison.

"I love camellias," Alison assured her. The older woman's eyes were bright, and the corners of her mouth turned up in a mysterious little bow. Alison wondered fleetingly if Jack had broken their news early. She handed Samantha a glass of sherry while Grace took the flowers and plopped them into a vase. They were eating in the kitchen because the rest of the house was too hard to de-dog.

"I'll say good night now," Grace told everyone. She had her hand on the door to go upstairs.

"Won't you join us for dinner?" Alison asked.

Grace shook her head. "Danny called this morning. He said he was sorry and that he wanted to come home. I told him the house was empty and he was welcome to it."

"Grace!"

"Well, I couldn't let him come back too easily," Grace said softly. She hitched her head a notch. "He hurt me. I want him back, but not unless he wants to be back. So, he's taking me to dinner tonight. Don't wait up; I may be late." She added the last with a wink that was so unlike Grace that Alison felt her mouth drop open.

"The child is beginning to develop some spark, just in time, I might add," Samantha noted.

"Grace isn't a child," Jamie said.

"Anyone under fifty is a child to me," Samantha told him as she patted his cheek. "Where'd you get the swell cup?"

"Alison," Jamie said. "She brought it to me with this." He dug in his pocket and emerged with a dirty ball of white and black fur.

Samantha studied it for a second. "Ah, a panda. That was nice of her."

"She loves me," Jamie said matter-of-factly. "Alison? Can I go out to the garage and see Nora?"

"You can go feed her, but try not to touch her much, okay?"

" 'Cause it will make Grandma Sam sneeze?"

"That's right. Hurry now—Jack's dinner is almost ready. It's very windy, so put on your jacket."

Jamie slammed the door behind him. Jack and Alison exchanged a bemused smile.

"You two keep grinning at each other," Samantha observed.

Jack looked at Alison. She nodded. "We're getting married," Jack announced. "Right here in this house."

Samantha gasped. "Oh, wonderful!" A delighted smile spread across her face. "Have you called your folks and your brothers? They'll all come for the wedding, won't they?" She stopped to think, and a frown crossed her face. "Does Jamie know? I mean, about you two."

"Not yet," Jack said. "I think he'll be pleased."

Samantha looked down at her hands quickly, but she didn't say anything. She didn't have to. Her silence screamed at Alison, who asked quietly, "Do you think there will be a problem?"

The older woman looked up and then away, her eyes uncomfortable. "How do I know? I just wonder if he'll be able to accept having to share the two of you. What's that fancy counselor of his say?"

"He sees her only once a month now," Jack said, "but I called her this morning. She foresees no problems."

Samantha shrugged. "What do I know? I'm just a silly old woman."

"You're hardly that," Jack said firmly, but he held Alison close against his side as he spoke. "Don't worry, either of you. Jamie will be delighted."

"Are you sure?" Alison asked, turning to look up into his eyes.

He grinned and reestablished the boundaries of her world. "Trust me. Now, call the little guy while I put dinner on the table, and don't say a word to him about this. Later, tonight—"

"Yes," Alison agreed, but the niggling worry that had been her second reaction when Jack asked her to marry him was back.

During dinner Samantha said, "Oh, by the way, I have news too."

Alison smiled. She had decided to put her doubts out of her mind for the time being. "I could tell you had something cooking the second you walked in here," she told Samantha.

"Well, you were right. I made a long-distance call today—to Moscow, of all places!

Took me a couple of operators but only one and a half minutes to be connected. Amazing, isn't it?"

"And?" Jack prompted.

"Oh. Well, I spoke with Nadia Gerasimov, my stepdaughter!"

Jack's mouth opened, but he didn't say a word.

"I never dreamed I'd see the day you were speechless, young man," Samantha said. "Do you realize my stepdaughter is only six years younger than I? Isn't that a hoot? Thank goodness she speaks excellent English. She's got a touch of rheumatism, though, and a new great-grandchild, so I'm the one going to make the trip late this summer."

"Gram!"

"Oh, yes. Nadia is so interested in hearing about Leo, don't you know? Well, of course she would be. After all, Leo was her father. And I want to see her. I think Leo would have liked that."

"Yes," Alison agreed softly. She took Samantha's hand in her own.

Jack refilled the water glasses. "A toast," he proposed, "to all good news everywhere."

"And to families," Samantha added.

Jamie giggled as they all touched glasses.

Alison was just getting ready to start clearing the table when she heard the front doorbell.

"I wonder . . ." she began but stopped when the bell rang twice more in rapid succession.

Jack started to get up, but Alison put her hand on his arm and rose. She was halfway down the hall when it rang again.

"Coming," she mumbled under her breath.

She opened the door, then hung on as the wind pushed it back into the house. The trees outside moaned and rustled. The outside lamp cast a bright light onto the porch. No one was there.

She stepped outside, holding her skirt down with one hand and her hair out of her mouth with the other. "Is anyone out here?"

A shape detached itself from the shadows and stepped into the light.

"Courtney!"

"May I come in?" Courtney shouted over the wind. She didn't wait for an answer but moved quickly past Alison into the hall.

Alison followed, tugging, then pushing the door closed against the brewing storm.

Courtney was wearing a long green wool coat cinched tight around her slender waist. Her hair was a mad tangle of apricot, her eyes wide. She held out a trembling hand, then snatched it back before Alison could touch her.

"What is it?" Alison asked. "Are you hurt?"

"No," Courtney said at once. She was regaining her inbred composure. She took a deep breath and looked up the stairs, then over her shoulder, down the hall. "Is Professor Foxx here?"

"Right here," Jack said. He'd come through the living room. Courtney's nervousness had so infected Alison that she joined Courtney in jumping at the sound of Jack's voice.

"Professor Foxx, I have to talk to you," Courtney said as she rushed forward to meet Jack. "I—well, I guess I just don't know what to do."

Jack took Courtney's arm and glanced at Alison, who shook her head. "Let's go into the den," he suggested.

"It's my mother," Courtney began before the three of them had even entered the room. "She is so stubborn!" She tore herself away from Jack and shook her hands in frustration. "There's only one way to do anything. *Her* way!"

"But Barton—" Alison protested.

"Barton. Humph! He likes my mother! They see eye to eye on practically everything. Living with him will be like an extension of living with her, and I can't handle it."

"Sit down," Jack invited. He pointed to a

deep plush chair, held out his hand to steady Courtney, then withdrew it, casting a helpless look toward Alison.

"Maybe you're having premarital jitters," Alison suggested.

Courtney plopped down in the chair. "I don't think so," she said thoughtfully as she drew a deep, steadying breath. "I've been rushed into this wedding all along. Mother didn't like Rob—you remember him, don't you, Professor Foxx?" Jack nodded and Courtney added, "Well, she broke us up and invited Barton to the house for the Christmas holidays, and I fell into her trap like an unwitting fly."

Alison laughed softly. Both Jack and Courtney looked at her with surprise.

"Sorry," she said, "but, Courtney, I just can't cast you in the role of the hapless victim. You're not a child. Take charge of your life."

"But Rob can't afford to get married right now. . . ."

"Then wait till he can afford it. Get a job. Earn a living. Go back to school. Get an apartment with a friend of yours to cut costs. Anything."

Courtney gave a snobbish laugh that petered out before it left her lips.

"Do you understand what she's saying?" Jack said kindly.

"That I should grow up?" Courtney ventured.

"Exactly." Jack patted her shoulder.

"I wouldn't know how to get a job." Courtney looked down at her feet. "I really don't know how to do anything."

"Come into the shop tomorrow, and I'll help," Alison said. "For that matter, I'm going to need someone for several months. Maybe you'd—"

"Me! Work in a flower shop!"

Alison laughed. "Yes, Courtney, you."

This time Courtney laughed. She took another deep breath and rose. "I'll come."

"By nine o'clock?"

"I don't usually get up till ten. Okay, okay, I'll be there."

Jack led her out of the room while Alison sank down into the vacated chair. "Deanne is going to kill me," she said, smiling to herself, imagining the look on her friend's face when she found out Courtney Howell was going to work at Two Hearts Florist!

Later, after everyone had gone home and it was just the three of them, Alison sat on the side of Jamie's bed and took his warm hand in hers. Nora was asleep on the end of the bed—

a special treat for suffering the indignity of being locked in the garage all evening. Jack stood over Alison, his hands on her shoulders. Outside the wind howled in the trees, but inside the house it was still and quiet as Alison and Jack studied Jamie's face, waiting for his response to their announcement.

"Then will you be my dad?" Jamie asked Jack.

Alison felt Jack's grip tighten. "Yes, son, I will," he said, his voice thick with emotion.

The little boy turned his attention to Alison. "And you'll still be my mom?"

Alison felt chills radiate through her chest, branching like ice water into her arms and legs and up her spine. "Yes," she whispered. "I'll always be your mom."

Jamie smiled slowly, sleepily as he wrapped his fingers around hers. Alison looked up at Jack, her eyes awash in tears, her throat choked. He leaned down and gently kissed her lips.